LAMPREYS

ALAN SPENCER

Chapter One

Dr. Chan feared this day would come.

Research termination.

The assistant director of PROJECT EV-180 PREY nervously paced the private conference room. One question burdened Dr. Chan's thoughts. How could she ensure the safety of hundreds of scientists and lower level lab techs? The team was drawing close to a successful end to the project, but the way things had been going lately, PROJECT EV-180 PREY would have to be put on hold or altogether terminated. The risk of public contamination was also becoming a serious threat.

Things were getting too dangerous too fast. Up to date, five people were missing on the top secret installation. The missing persons' whereabouts were still unknown. Worse yet, there was a fatality this morning. One of the lab techs, Edward Campbell, didn't report for morning duty. They discovered Campbell's private quarters splattered in blood. Shards of bones were embedded in the walls and parts of Edward were left behind in chewed up pieces.

Dr. Chan had opened up many specimens on her lab tables over the course of twenty-seven years in the global/marine research business, but she'd never seen anything this gruesome. The project was ambitious and demanded sacrifices, but Campbell's death drove her to take Dr. Sutherland aside and convince him to put the staff on lockdown until further notice. The director of PROJECT EV-180 PREY had to listen to reason. Everybody was in immediate danger, and Dr. Sutherland had to make the right call when proceeding with these delicate matters.

"You saw Dr. Campbell's room, didn't you?" Dr. Chan begged Dr. Sutherland to take this seriously. "Campbell looked like his body was sent through a blender. Only one thing on this installation could've done that kind of damage to a person. We have to lockdown everybody, contain the escaped subjects, and retool the project. I don't even know who released the subjects in the first place."

Were her words sinking into the stubborn director's head? What the hell was wrong with Dr. Sutherland lately? His bold white hair was out of its ponytail and hanging wildly about his shoulders. A curious smile was drawn on his haggard face. What was Dr. Sutherland thinking about?

"Dr. Campbell was a good man," Dr. Sutherland said, breaking the long-held awkward silence between them. "Maybe not a great scientist, Campbell, but every research team needs its pencil pushers. But his death will contribute to the cause. That's what matters. No human life is too great a price."

Dr. Chan was mortified hearing the response. "Who are you? Can you hear yourself? I want you to lock down the base and call in for help. This is beyond our control. We'll all die like Campbell if we don't. If you won't do it, so help me God, I'll call ENTECH myself and go over your head. I'll them how you've lost your mind. This was only supposed to last a year, and PROJECT EV-180 PREY has gone on for three *long* years. You need to get off this installation and get your head back on straight. Frankly, doctor, I question your sanity."

Had Dr. Sutherland heard a single word she'd been saying?

Didn't he understand the urgency of the matter?

"Nothing is too great a price to see this project to its full conclusion," Dr. Sutherland said in a disturbing monotone. "I'm in constant contact with our superiors. Everything is as it should be. Deaths will occur. ENTECH is willing to pay that price. This is what the company wants. This is what Mama wants too."

"Excuse me? Who is Mama?"

"You haven't met Mama. She's above your clearance level, good doctor."

Dr. Chan couldn't stand how matter-of-factly the director was talking about these matters of life and death. "If ENTECH knows this is going on, then why aren't they helping us? Are they planning to let these things have their way with the staff? Did you let the lampreys out of their tanks, Dr. Sutherland? My God, if that's true, then how long have they been free?"

Dr. Sutherland couldn't contain that knowing grin.

"The lampreys have had free rein since the beginning. They were just waiting for the right time to feed. Mama knows when the time is right. They're only getting hungrier, Dr. Chan, and what we're feeding them in the labs isn't enough. Fish guts and pig brains won't cut it anymore. So, the only right thing to do, good doctor, is to give them what they want, and that's meat, pounds and pounds of it. It's the only way to see their true potential. We must all die in the name of science."

A chunk of the ceiling collapsed right above Dr. Chan's head. She dodged the falling debris after unleashing a scream. Next, she heard banging and drumming above in the duct system. It sounded like a sledgehammer bashing against sheet metal. The noises were coming closer and closer. Then Dr. Chan heard something else. She imagined bone grinding against bone.

Crick-clack-crick-clack-crick-clack-crick-clack-crick-clack.

Dr. Chan was paralyzed. She couldn't take her eyes off the large gaping hole in the ceiling. She could only see darkness staring back at her.

"Come and get it!" Dr. Sutherland invited. "I know you're hungry. We're all so...very...hungry. ENTECH's given you free rein. Show us your full potential."

Something horrific happened to Dr. Sutherland's face. His eyes rolled into the back of his head. The eyes literally fell back into his skull. The sockets were now empty pink holes. Around the circumference of his eyes, jagged teeth sprouted. The teeth were long enough for light to reflect against the off-white veneers. Then the teeth retracted and Dr. Sutherland's eyes rolled back up into the sockets.

"They got to you," Dr. Chan gasped, "but how? What did they do to you? They can't think for themselves. They can't infect us. We didn't create them to do anything else, except—no, *nooooooooooooo!*"

The banging stopped right above Dr. Chan. The dark hole in the ceiling was replaced by a writhing tube of gray meat. The subject's maw was the size of a manhole cover. Jagged teeth sprouted around the circumference of the circle mouth, protracting for the kill. Rubber glue saliva pelted Dr. Chan in thick wads.

Those deadly teeth spun in a circular motion at high speeds. A motor's whine echoed down to her; the song of her impending death.

The walls of the subject's inner body created a suction. That suction forced Dr. Chan's long black hair to stand up on end. She reached to grab onto something to anchor herself in place, but her feet were already up off the ground. Her arms shot up involuntarily over her head. Screaming did no good, but she did so anyway. Her peals were loud enough to rip the paint from the walls. Launching up to the ceiling, Dr. Chan was sucked up into the subject's mouth.

Dr. Sutherland stood by and watched her body vanish into the ceiling. The rewarding sound of bone teeth shredding through flesh soon followed. Swirling jets of crimson splattered everything in a few yard's radius of the kill zone. Dr. Chan was nothing more than matter to be digested and excreted.

"I knew you were hungry," Dr. Sutherland said out loud. "So am I. Our appetites are insatiable."

Dr. Sutherland exited the private conference room. He casually walked down three halls to his private office. There, he watched a wall of TVs playing monitor feeds from every room in the installation. Those who didn't know the situation would soon find out what was happening. That gave the doctor very little time to act. He worked the security system. He locked down every exit out of the research installation.

Nobody was leaving.

It was time to feed.

Chapter Two

Conrad Garfield heard knocking and had zero interest in answering the front door. Early afternoon sunlight bled through the curtains of his apartment. Conrad glanced at his digital clock. It was already past noon. Conrad didn't care. The new semester at Texas University started in two weeks. He resigned from his job as an English professor last semester. That was after his disastrous wedding. The ceremony was the biggest blunder of his life. The video shot at the wedding reception of his wife was an Internet sensation, and Conrad's ultimate humiliation. Conrad still didn't know who posted that video. He imagined it was probably one of his ex-wife's dumbass friends.

The knocking stopped. Conrad stayed in bed. A moment passed when he thought the person would go away, but then Conrad heard the key turning in the door. Only one person had a spare key.

Oh no, not now.

Conrad heard his brother and father talking to each other as they burst into his apartment. First, it was Duke, his older brother, saying, "God, this place is a disaster area. There's trash everywhere. If I realized Conrad was taking it this hard, I would've stepped in a long time ago."

Then his dad, Henry, defending Conrad, said, "A man needs time alone after he gets his balls crushed."

Henry raised his voice. "Conrad, where are you? You still in bed? Come on out, son. We need to talk."

"I'll be right there," Conrad said. His voice was heavy with sleep and a hangover. "Wait for me in the living room. You guys should've called first."

"So you can hide your shame?" Duke laughed. "You're keeping Keno's Pizza in business. There's like ten empty boxes stacked up here. And you haven't been drinking alone, have you? Or are you just collecting empty bourbon bottles?" Under Duke's breath, "*Arielle really did a number on the poor guy. It's almost a good thing this worked out like it did. Conrad needs to get out of his head.*"

Conrad threw on a t-shirt and basketball shorts, and rubbed the sleep out of his face. He stumbled on a 2-liter bottle of soda, took a swig, and gagged. The soda was flat. He would need more than flat soda to take in what his family would soon ask him to do.

Duke was studying the living room with disdain playing on his face. He was shaking his head and passing judgments. Henry, on the other hand, was sitting on the couch thumbing through the scrapbook Conrad and Arielle had made over the two years they had dated. Conrad felt the heat of tears rush to his eyes.

How was he ever going to get over Arielle?

Henry invited Conrad to sit down. When Conrad did, Duke walked to the fridge. "All you eat is crap, Conrad. How do you expect to feel better when all you're eating is junk?"

"Duke, enough," Henry said. "We're here to talk to Conrad, not judge him. We need his help, remember?"

"He's going to say no, because he's a little bitch. You want to take him along, go ahead, but I'm not going to be changing his tampon the whole time. Conrad can't handle himself. He's not a physical guy. He likes to read and pontificate, whatever the fuck that means."

"He might want to come along," Henry said. "Now would you sit down and shut up, Duke?"

Duke and Henry's father/son relationship was much like a drill sergeant/cadet. They both served time in the military. Father and son were both wearing khaki pants and button up shirts. Both of their heads were buzzed. Conrad's hair was long and in a ponytail, and his clothes were as dressed down as possible. Even growing up, Conrad was different from his father and brother. Conrad read Faulkner, Twain, Keats, and Steinbeck, while Duke was out shooting small arms and semi-automatics at the local firing range with his dad. Duke and Henry shared a subscription to *Guns & Ammo*. They hunted deer on the weekends, while Conrad stayed home and hung out with his mother. Duke and Conrad were polar opposites. That's why it was strange they were trying to include Conrad in something that appeared to be physically challenging and out of Conrad's wheelhouse.

Conrad couldn't help but ask, "What is this about?"

Henry closed the photo scrapbook. "You need to get over Arielle. We know what she did was bad, but I'm not going to watch you get any worse. You need to call her a bitch and move on."

"What she did wasn't just *bad*." Duke scoffed. "The bitch got so drunk at the wedding, she went through a laundry list of the people she'd slept with while dating Conrad. And man, it was a *long* list. I think I checked my watch a few times waiting for her to get to the end."

Conrad's pulse was pounding hard. The same anger and humiliation on his wedding day hit him again fresh. "You guys don't understand. Arielle humiliated me, and everybody, including you two guys, laughed at me. My friends, my co-workers at the university, even the dean, were all there to see it happen. I quit my job, because Arielle works in the English department. It's embarrassing. I can't see her, and I can't see everybody else either."

Duke's smile was growing on his face. He hadn't heard a single word Conrad had just said. "I remember that toast before you guys were supposed to cut the wedding cake. Arielle was sloshed as hell, man. How could you not laugh? Arielle said she wanted to, "Have her cake and fuck it too." I mean, *damn*."

"Duke, enough." Henry picked up an empty bottle of bourbon. "You've been drinking, Conrad. You didn't used to be a drinker."

"I'm an adult," Conrad said. "I can do whatever I want."

"I know you're an adult, and I know how you get sometimes. You do that things writers and creative types do. They drink, they look inwards, they go in too deep, and they don't come out of the darkness. Who's that tragic writer guy? Edgar Allan Poe, that's the guy. You don't want to end up like Poe? Didn't he fall into something and die? I can't remember. Anyway, you need a fresh start, and you're not getting it in this apartment. So what if Arielle screwed you over? Thank God, you two didn't have kids. It could be worse, Conrad. You have a good life, son. I want you to realize that."

"I loved her," Conrad said. "I was ready for kids. I was ready for it all."

"She was out blowing dudes while you were keeping house," Duke blurted out. "Snap out of it. She no longer has control over you. You're a free man."

"It's been two months," Henry said. "You haven't called home. We check in on you, and all you do is stay in this apartment and wallow. And I didn't know you quit your job."

"Arielle's in the English department," Conrad said, defending his decision. "I can't see her, because I'm still in love with her."

"It's amazing what women can do to us," Duke said. "She's out of your life, and she's still got your balls in a vice. Look, Conrad, you're my brother, but it's time to take back your balls."

"Enough about my balls!"

Conrad stomped across the room, stood in front of the screen door room, and looked outside. He needed a break from his family's interrogation.

Henry got up, turned Conrad around, and gave him a hug. "I love you, Conrad. Forget everything we're saying. It's your life. You do what you need to do to get better, but you need to come up for air. Will you hear us out?"

Duke had picked up a copy of the Charles Dickens novel *Hard Times* that was on the kitchen table between two giant piles of literary books. Duke eyed the book as if he expected it to be a *Hustler*, and he instead got an issue of *Southern Living*.

"You going to tell him what's up, Dad?"

Henry invited Conrad to sit back down on the couch. Conrad would be glad he was sitting, because he would've fallen over after hearing what was coming his way.

"We've both done our time in the service, as you know," Henry explained. "I was in Vietnam, and Duke served in Iraq. It's okay that you're not into what we do, Conrad. I appreciate the differences between you and your brother. I apologize if it seems like I'm closer to Duke."

Duke was shifting in his chair. He was on the verge of words and kept cutting himself off. It was making Conrad nervous the way they were both acting.

"Sometimes ex-military get called upon to do side jobs by private companies," Henry continued. "Sometimes it's government related, and other times, the jobs come from independent entities. These special jobs are few and far between. I have a crew of people I lead, and Duke's a member of that crew. It's important what we do, but it's also top secret. We're all close, because we've seen tough combat situations together. That's probably why I've formed special bonds with Duke that I don't have with you, Conrad. I have to work on that, and I have a solution for that problem."

Conrad's stomach kept dropping.

What were they trying to tell him?

"Do you guys want me to go on one of your secret missions? Do you guys fight terrorists in your spare time?"

Duke smiled. "Yeah, sometimes."

"We do jobs under the radar," Henry said. "Research companies run into problems, or the government doesn't want to allocate bigger resources to solve issues, so they use small teams of trusted people like us to complete odd jobs. We're small and effective teams. We get out and get the job done and shut up about it. Off the books, off the record."

"You guys never told me this before." Conrad's concern was growing. "I don't know what to say. So what do I have to do with this? You're not seriously asking me to get involved, are you?"

"One of our team members is out of commission. A skiing accident in Colorado. The guy broke his pelvis. Gibbons is out, so we've got an open seat. I need a quick replacement."

Conrad suddenly felt nauseous. He leaned forward, took a breath, and braced himself for more information. "Me? I can't even look at a gun, never mind fire one."

Duke threw up his hands. "Are you certain we should be telling him about what we do?"

"He's your brother, and he's a member of the family. He should've known a long time ago. Your mom's always said that, and she was right. Conrad's fine. I'm not asking you to shoot a gun, buddy. I'm not even asking you to enter a hot zone. This is a humanitarian gig. It's a volunteer job. We're going to Africa. We're going to be digging ditches and working on creating a clean water supply in the village of—"

"Wait, I still don't understand what you guys do," Conrad said. "Do you seriously go after terrorists? And *Mom* knows?"

Henry grabbed Conrad's arm. His father didn't want Conrad to blow his top. "Yes, your mom knows. Listen to me. It doesn't matter what we do, necessarily. It's nothing you have to worry about. This is a humanitarian job we're talking about. It doesn't pay money. It's not like our other gigs. It's a mission of peace. Don't worry about what else we do otherwise. That's our burden to shoulder.

"You need to come up for air, Conrad. A big dose of perspective will show you your life isn't all that bad. Other people have it a lot worse than we do. I'm not watching my son feel sorry for himself a moment longer. I want to include you in a family tradition; at least the volunteer stuff. Your grandfather did this kind of work after World War II. A few of your uncles do this work too, and I just wanted to include you, Conrad. You might like it, or you might not, and it's no big deal if you don't. I'm asking you a favor this one time. We're under the gun here. The opportunity happened a week ago. A private group offered to pay for tickets, lodging, and meals in exchange for our labor. I got all of our crew to sign up. The job's tomorrow. One seat's open, and your name is on it."

"Tomorrow?"

Duke pointed at the pizza boxes. "What, you doing something tomorrow?"

"I'm still not over the fact you guys are mercenaries or whatever."

"We're not mercenaries on this trip," Henry said. "Hey, we've got a free plane ticket to Africa. It'd hate to see it go to waste because Gibbons broke his pelvis."

"Africa? I-I don't know, guys."

That judgmental grin spread on Duke's face. "See, Dad, I told you he didn't want his balls back. Arielle neutered him."

"*Fuck you.*" Conrad was going to push Duke off of his chair. Duke sidestepped him, and Conrad was slammed into the carpet. Duke had Conrad's arm pulled behind his back. Four pressure points delivered white hot pain into Conrad's body.

"Say yes," Duke demanded. "Dad tried to ask the nice way. You're acting like a little bitch. You need to get over yourself. A trip to Africa will do you some good. Maybe if you do this, instead of reading stories, you'll actually have your own stories to tell. So quit bleeding out your ass and say yes. Help someone out for a change that is less fortunate than you."

The pain was so intense, Conrad begged his brother to let him go. He said yes ten times before Duke finally released him.

Henry helped Conrad up to his feet and sat him in the chair. "Why did you do that? He's your brother. You're not supposed to fight."

Conrad had a question after rotating his arm a few times. "How come you guys never told me about these jobs before?"

Henry shook his head. "You tell him, Duke."

Duke picked up the novel *The Grapes of Wrath* from the floor and tossed it across the room like a Frisbee. "Because, brother, you're kind of a wimp."

Chapter Three

Conrad was alone in his apartment after being told he was going to board a plane the next morning at five. The destination, Africa. Henry told him the volunteer mission was located in a city in Chad called Faya-Largeau. The group would help build housing, work on creating a clean water source, deliver medical aide, and meet natives and promote peace.

What kind of work did his family really do? They were so vague about that information. He pictured his family going to odd places smoking out war criminals, terrorists, and acting as hit men for the highest bidder. Maybe being out of the loop was for his benefit, he decided.

Conrad spent the rest of the afternoon straightening up his apartment. Then he started searching for new jobs. He quit his teaching job at Texas University after the botched wedding and Arielle's public confession. He could look into the local community college for adjunct work, or perhaps a gig out of the city. Maybe a change in scenery would do him some good.

His family was right.

He needed to come up for air.

The idea of going to Africa was starting to sink in, and he was starting to like it. Conrad was single, unemployed, and ready for whatever life had in store for him next. People did have it worse than him out there. He had easy access to running water, food, and he wasn't being shot at on a daily basis. Conrad remembered hearing stories about war criminals in Liberia hacking off people's hands up to the elbow with machetes. The term "short sleeves" used in the article mortified him. His family worked to take care of the scum responsible for crimes against humanity. Whether it was on the books or off the books, bad guys existed, and they needed cleaning up.

So what if Arielle got plowed at their wedding and confessed her sins to everybody? The situation was miniscule against real world problems. Sure, it was bad. Fifteen people she'd slept with was the final count. Then she asked the crowd if sleeping with women counted because there wasn't any penetration. This all happened after Arielle had almost chugged an entire bottle of sparkling champagne by herself. The threat of monogamy was too much for her to handle.

I'm a gypsy spirit, words from Arielle's speech. *My parents had an open marriage. Why can't we, Conrad? It doesn't mean I don't love you. It means I love you even more. Every guy I slept with, it reminded me of how great you are. This is how I want to live my life. I want to have my cake and fuck it too.*

After that was said, Arielle slammed down a piece of their wedding cake between her legs. Then she vomited. Arielle's sister helped her into the bathroom, and that was the end of the wedding. They hadn't signed the official marriage certificate. The wedding was cancelled. After that, Conrad stayed in his apartment cooped up like a victim.

The time for mourning a failed marriage was over.

Duke said he should stop bleeding out his ass, and Conrad agreed.

Conrad stormed about the apartment taking down photos of him and Arielle together. It was over now and forever.

"Forget the tramp," he said. "The bitch is done."

After filling up a box of relationship mementos, he threw the oversized scrapbook on top of the pile.

"No more wallowing. It's time to move on and clean the slate."

Conrad left the apartment and headed straight for the garbage bin. It was a stand-alone bin in the corner of the parking lot. Conrad held the box in his hands for a moment, and then he tossed the box in the trash.

He was freed from Arielle's curse.

Conrad marched back to his apartment with a better disposition. Life wasn't going to conquer him; *he* was going to conquer life.

The man sitting at his kitchen table pointing a 9mm at Conrad's chest quickly soured his good mood.

Chapter Four

The man aiming the 9mm at Conrad was named Amati. Amati was dressed in black pants and a brown aviation jacket. His black hair was slicked back, and his finely trimmed beard made him look like a cross between a military man and a mob goon.

Amati's eyes were sharp and critical sizing up Conrad. "So you're Conrad Garfield?"

Conrad stood there in the living room unsure of what to say. "*Um*, yes."

"Duke and Henry can come out of the worst of situations on the field with a few scratches and bruises, but you; you're nothing more than an out-of-shape English professor. You sure swam out of a different end of the gene pool, my friend. This is going to work out nicely."

"What do you want from me?" Conrad asked. "How do you know my family?"

"You really know very little about what your family does. I've been keeping close watch over them during the past few days. It's fortunate that things are coming together like they are. You're going to make me a rich man. We've got a serious situation on our hands, and only Henry and his team can help."

"You mean in Africa?"

Amati's piercing eyes bored into Conrad. "They're not going to Africa. Sorry, unpack your bags, buddy. This other mission is much more important. You're my little piece of insurance to make sure Henry's team gets out there, they do their job, and they do it fast. If they can't do it, nobody else will. Twelve of the best teams have already been slaughtered where you're going. Trust me, I've seen the pictures. Messy shit, my friend, but those guys were amateurs compared to your father."

Conrad felt the room grow hotter. "This is too much. I need to sit down."

Amati pointed his gun at the couch. "Have a seat then."

The man was having a good time watching Conrad have a small breakdown. Amati kept shaking his head and whispering things under his breath. *"This guy."* *"Unbelievable."*

There was a stretch of silence. Conrad wanted to feel the guy out. Was he in immediate danger? "Are you making my family kill terrorists?"

Amati's left eyebrow shifted inquisitively. "You really don't know anything about what your family does, do you? Let me learn you a few things, pal. Your father's in charge of assembling and training tactical teams. I'm in charge of getting those tactical teams jobs. Your father's teams have gone to Afghanistan, Pakistan, Istanbul," he laughed, "and that one incident in South Dakota. If only people knew! I almost got them onto the team that took out Osama Bin Laden. Your father helps me put together capable teams to take out high level threats. You can only image what we've accomplished."

Conrad rubbed his aching head. "Why go through the trouble of taking me as hostage, if my family works for you and all, right?"

Amati was bored with talking. "It's simple. The people I work for didn't want to give your father a chance to say no to the mission. They should've picked him first, but our teams don't work for cheap. You get what you pay for, in my opinion."

"I can't believe this."

"Get over it," Amati said. "I got you a change of clothes. They're sitting on your bed."

"For what?"

"Don't worry. Go into your room and get dressed. Then we're going for a ride."

Conrad couldn't feel his body. He was so nervous. There were things happening he didn't understand. Whatever his family did in secret, he was being pulled right in.

The clothing on top of the bed was black boots, black pants, black shirt, and a pocket vest.

Conrad was hesitant to undress.

Amati smiled. "I won't look. The last thing I want to see is your naked lily-white ass. Now get on with it. We've got a schedule to keep."

Conrad put on the clothes.

"What's in this vest?"

"A few things you might need on the field."

"But I'm not a solider? I'm an English Professor."

"It doesn't matter what you are. If something happens, you should have a fighting chance."

Conrad was about to dig through the pockets when Amati pressed the gun to his chest. Seething mad, he growled, "You don't open any of those pockets until I tell you so. You follow my every instruction, or I kill you, then I kill your family. Your brother and your father might be a tall order, but I know where your mother lives. I can make the call and have someone shoot her where she stands. You want that?"

"No, of course not!"

"Good. I'm going to lead you outside to a vehicle. I can't walk in broad daylight flashing my gun, now can I? I need to know you're not going to cause any problems. You go where I say you go. Say nothing to nobody. Got it?"

Conrad agreed. He was sweating profusely. Nerves he didn't know existed were amped up. Arielle and being unemployed were meaningless problems up against the Amati situation.

Amati led him out the front door. A neighbor across the hall opened her door. It was Gertrude Smith. She was a sweet old lady who kept asking about "that pretty girl" who used to come over all the time.

Gertrude said hello.

Conrad did his best to play it cool.

"Gertrude, good afternoon."

"It's a nice day," Gertrude said. "Say, I haven't seen that pretty girl around lately. Is she okay? You've looked kind of down lately. A handsome young man like you should be soaking up sunshine and living life. You only live once, Conrad. You haven't done anything to lose that girl, have you?"

You old biddy, can you drop the subject? I already told you we divorced, even though it's none of your business.

"We're not together anymore, but she's doing fine," Conrad said. "My friend and I are about to go out. I'm late, for um, a lunch reservation. I'll talk to you later."

Conrad imagined Amati whipping out that gun and plugging three rounds center masse into Gertrude's chest, then one in the head, to make sure she didn't tell anyone about the hostage situation.

"I have to go, Gertrude. We'll talk later, okay? I promise."

Gertrude kept smiling. "I'll hold you to it."

They broke away from Gertrude.

Amati was telling Conrad to walk away from the apartment complex and towards the parking lot. There wasn't very many people around at this time of the day. A white van pulled up. The sliding door came open. Conrad couldn't process the moment. The two goons, dressed in black combat gear, wrestled Conrad into the van. They had him on the floor. They used plastic twine to secure his hands together behind his back. Amati sat in the passenger seat, while a woman drove fast from the parking lot.

"Keep your head down," one of the goons said. "Act like you're dead until we tell you you're not dead anymore."

Conrad did as he was told and played dead.

Chapter Five

The van traveled many miles to an unknown destination. Nobody in the van was talking. There was a tension Conrad couldn't put his finger on. The way Amati talked about Duke and Henry, Amati respected them, and he also feared them. Amati had worked with Henry in the past. Would this hostage situation be enough to win his family's compliance in whatever mission, or did Amati fear retaliation?

A dreadful thought slipped into Conrad's head.

What if he was killed in the process of this transaction?

He knew so little about Duke and Henry's special assignments. So many things could happen, and Conrad wouldn't see it coming.

The van stopped. Two persons helped Conrad to his feet. Amati was already out of the van waiting. They were parked outside a cheap hotel at the edge of town. It was the kind of hotel that offered hourly rates. Two strip clubs were located to the left of the Sun Motel called *Bazookas* and *The Rumpus Room*. Conrad didn't want to ask them what they were doing *here* of all places. They were at least fifty miles from his apartment.

Amati unlocked the door to Room 4. Two men and one woman stared at Amati awaiting his orders. Amati pointed at the wooden chair in the corner of the room. "Sit him down there. Fryer, you get your camera ready. Keyes, tie him to the chair. We don't want the motherfucker falling out of his chair."

"Wait, before you gag him," Amati said. "Have you eaten anything in the past few hours?"

Conrad cleared his dry throat. "No, I haven't had anything to eat today."

"When was your last bowel movement?"

"*What?*"

"When did you last take a shit?" Keyes reiterated. "Answer the man."

"This morning."

"Bavardi, get ready to take care of Conrad. Fryer, gag him, and make sure it's in right. I don't want this asshole choking to death. If he's dead, this mission is ruined. Consider yourselves terminated. Henry will scour the earth for our heads."

Bavardi was the biggest of the group. Conrad imagined if Sylvester Stallone and Ed Gein had somehow morphed into one body builder sociopath, you would have Bavardi.

Fryer was the tall and lanky one in the group. Keyes, the woman, grabbed Bavardi by his thick bicep. "Now don't go too crazy. You don't want to kill him. You know what happened last time we tied somebody up and worked them over. It took over an hour to clean up after you."

Fryer stuffed folded up socks into Conrad's mouth and covered his lips with a swatch of duct tape. "Just pace yourself. I'm not cleaning up a bunch of blood this time. I shouldn't need more than one towel, you got me?"

Bavardi huffed before slipping on a pair of black gloves. He flexed his fists and studied Conrad. "Stop worrying, Fryer. I know what I'm doing."

"This is going to hurt, my friend," Bavardi said to Conrad with a sly grin. "I'm not going to lie. Whenever you have bad dreams, you'll see this room, you'll see me, and you'll be feeling this all over again. I will be your recurring nightmare."

Fryer was recording Conrad in the chair with a video camera in his hands. Amati was making calls on his cell phone. Keyes watched Bavardi as if she was ready to hold the man back at a moment's notice.

Conrad's body swelled with terror. He knew what was coming, and there wasn't a damn thing he could do about it.

He couldn't even call out for help.

Chapter Six

Bavardi went outside for air. The man was in a rage. Fryer and Amati had to restrain him moments ago. Bavardi wanted to keep pummeling Conrad with his fists. The man went all-out psychotic. Conrad thought the man was going to kill him. The fists just kept coming. Now that the situation had calmed, Fryer stopped recording and started taking pictures of Conrad's ugly face. Five punches Bavardi had inflicted up on him. They were mean, thundering blows. Conrad knew this because Bavardi counted out loud. Each count was a thrilling declaration.

Fryer finished taking pictures of Conrad. Keyes knelt down next to Conrad. She looked at him with her pretty green eyes and sympathetic face. "Your nose is probably broken. Your left eye might swell shut. Your bottom lip is split and bleeding. You probably feel like you got hit by a freight train. Just know it's over. Your part of it's done."

Conrad would later learn that was a big lie.

Keyes removed the gag. Conrad involuntarily spit blood down his chin. He'd ready many novels where people get interrogated by cheesy detectives, cleaned up by mobsters, or robbed at gunpoint. Words couldn't describe what it was like to have the blood beaten out of your face.

Amati and Fryer were working together with a cell phone and a camera. Keyes had gone into the bathroom to gather up a few towels. She winced looking at Conrad's face as she dabbed the blood from his face.

"If it's any consolation, you took it pretty damn well. You might look like a huge pansy, but your father would be proud."

It slipped out of Conrad's mouth, "Fuck you."

Amati laughed. "He's his father's son."

"We just sent the pictures and video to Henry," Amati said. "Now we know everybody on Henry's team has met up at a Holiday Inn. They're lunching and talking about the upcoming trip to Africa. The timing's perfect. They're all together in one place when they'll see Conrad's busted face. Once they get this picture of Conrad's ugly mug, we could be in for some trouble. Henry could agree to our terms once he calls, or he could come after us and retaliate. Remember, we set the terms. We maintain control of the situation. We get Henry's team to the installation, and we're home free. Easy money."

Bavardi returned from outside. He smelled like a freshly smoked cigarette. The man had a different demeanor, as if he hadn't just ruthlessly punched out a helpless person. Everything was calm and good in the psycho's world.

Amati issued orders. Keyes and Fryer helped Conrad out of the chair. He was still wobbly on his feet and his head was full of pain. Moving outside, they laid out Conrad on the floor of the van. Everybody loaded in and they were driving. Once again, Conrad had no idea where the hell they were going.

Chapter Seven

"Henry received the pictures and video of Conrad on his phone," Amati said to everyone. "Henry will be calling any minute. I bet he's fucking pissed."

A cell phone rang right after Amati made the comment. After a heated discussion, Amati hung up the phone. "Henry agreed to meet us at the rendezvous point with his team. We could come up against some gunplay there. The best idea is to avoid any escalation. We state our terms, disarm Henry's team, and we get on that chopper that'll fly us to the private installation. Conrad is our collateral. Henry won't jeopardize his son's life. He's all the collateral we'll need. My hope is to get through this without a single bullet fired. So take this time to clear your minds and get your head in the game. This is the hard part of the job."

Conrad didn't like the silence. The silence made it too easy for concerns to spin in his head. How many different ways could Conrad die in this situation?

Many.

How many different ways could he live?

Few.

Conrad felt ridiculous wearing the vest, combat pants, and gear. Then it hit him what was going to happen. Why else would he wear combat gear of any kind? He was going to be forced into a fighting situation. Wherever Henry and his team were being forced to go, Conrad would be right there with them.

No, Conrad argued to himself. His father wouldn't let that happen, but then again, the man wasn't in control of the situation. Anything could happen, and nobody could stop it.

The van kept driving.

Conrad kept imagining the various and colorful methods he could die.

Chapter Eight

"Henry's real pissed," Amati kept saying to everyone. Conrad thought the man sounded scared. "But let's look on the bright side; I'm glad I'm not on the receiving end of this business deal. Henry's a good soldier, but shit, they don't know what they're up against. We still don't know what's going on in that installation, really. Either way, we've got Henry where we want him.

"When Henry saw the photos of your bloody veal face, Conrad, it sounded like he was ready to go on a rampage. That's why we can't be lazy. A split second is all it takes to make a mistake. Henry and his team will be going in hot. We stick to the plan. I expect everybody to be on top of it. You get me?"

Keyes, Fryer, and Bavardi each yelled, "Yes, sir!"

Conrad couldn't see any of them. He was still on the floor with his wrists tied behind his back. Keyes had her foot on the small of his back in case he tried to escape. After the speech, she pressed her foot down even harder.

The drive lasted a few more hours. Conrad was exhausted, and his head felt like a grenade had gone off inside his skull. Bavardi's snarling, mad dog expression as he pummeled Conrad with his unrelenting fists repeated itself in his head. These people weren't just mercenaries, guns for hire, or ex-military tactical teams, these were trained killers capable of doing a job without an ounce of remorse. Bavardi was a prime example of a tried and true killer. Conrad didn't want to deal with the mad bastard ever again.

Amati spoke up after a long stretch of silence.

"I don't want you guys to feel like you're double crossing anyone. This is a business just like any other. We create ties, and we break them all the same. Keep your eyes on the dollar signs. This is the biggest take I've ever had, and I know you guys haven't made this money in one shot before either. Henry trained us all for special combat. He did a job and he was paid for it. You don't owe him anything. This is business. Keep it that way, and you'll keep getting the better paying gigs. You can make money the hard way, and keep throwing yourself into the hot zone like Henry and Duke do, or you can fast track your way up the food chain and be like us. Or do you want to chase terrorists in caves for the rest of your careers like Henry's team does for chump change?"

Keyes, Fryer, and Bavardi laughed.

No, they didn't want to do the shit jobs for shit pay.

After roughly another hour, the van stopped. Conrad had no idea where they were now. Keyes hoisted Conrad from up off of the floor. It took a moment for Conrad's legs to be strong again. They wanted to buckle and drop him to the ground. He still didn't feel right after Bavardi's assault. Nausea came and went in waves. The nervous energy in his body refused to dissipate.

Duke had told Conrad about his time in Iraq one time. Duke would be pinned down by snipers, and he would stay awake for fourteen to twenty hours, if not longer. Duke started seeing things in the corner of his eyes that weren't there. He imagined voices telling he was going die a horrible death. Would that start happening to Conrad? Would paranoia and exhaustion do him in? How much longer before he cracked under the pressure of a bad situation?

Conrad's nose started bleeding again. It trailed across his lips and soaked into his already blood covered shirt. The pain in his face spread like a gasoline fire.

"Good, he's bleeding again," Amati said, noticing Conrad's face. "The worse he looks, the more likely they'll go along with the plan."

"I can do some touch up work," Bavardi chimed in when he also stepped out of the van. "He's not quite ugly enough. He should be wearing scars for the rest of his life. However long that may be."

Conrad's body tensed. Keyes laughed, sending out a girlish shrill. "He went stiff when you said that, Bavardi. He's scared shitless."

Bavardi's ice-cold eyes met Conrad's. Bavardi was face to face with Conrad. Conrad was trembling. What was coming his way next? The man was clearly psychotic, Conrad thought.

"If I had my way, I would've killed you earlier with my bare hands," Bavardi said. "You didn't say anything, you didn't fight back, and you didn't do anything at all to stop me. You're useless. You're nothing. You're a shame to your father. You should've been aborted the second you squirted out of your mother's pussy."

Looking back, Conrad would tell you it was the punches to the head that ruined his reasoning power. This wasn't an act of bravery; it was an act of temporary insanity.

Conrad growled through gritted teeth, "I should've been aborted, huh?"

Bavardi realized he had Conrad going. "Yeah, she should've done you a clothes hanger favor. Pussy, you're a— *ahhhhhhhhhhshit!*"

Conrad head butted Bavardi's nose. The blow was rewarded with a distinct snap. Blood was running down the bottom half of the angry man's face. Growling with the ferocity of a starving bear, Bavardi motioned to grab Conrad by the neck and throttle him.

"I'M GOING TO KILL YOU!!!"

Keyes jumped on Bavardi's back.

Her weight did nothing to stop the raging freight train.

"No, Bavardi!" Keyes shouted. She was all in a panic. She knew she couldn't contain the beast. "He's our hostage. He has to be alive. You can't kill him. Bavardi, listen to me. Bavardi! Don't fuck this up!"

Fryer, the taller, leaner version of Bavardi, wrenched Keyes off of Bavardi's back. Then Fryer tried to put Bavardi in a headlock, but Bavardi threw Fryer to one side and charged full on at Conrad. Conrad couldn't believe what he'd just done, and now the punishment was coming with interest due.

Conrad fell backwards, stumbling in fear, and landed on his back. His hands were tied by plastic twine, but his legs weren't. He crawled backwards to avoid Bavardi's backlash. It wasn't enough. Bavardi was on top of Conrad. Both his hands squeezed Conrad's neck. Bavardi's face was the color of freshly ground meat. Conrad couldn't stare incoming death in the face. He closed his eyes.

Bavardi was dripping blood from his nose onto Conrad's face. "Look at me. *I said look at me!*"

Conrad opened his eyes and made eye contact with the devil. Bavardi's sinister eyes seared into Conrad.

"Nobody does that to me and lives. Fear me, because no matter what happens, I will kill you. Not even your father can help you. I'll eat you alive and shit out your soul. I'll—"

"*Gaaaaah!*" Bavardi went stiff, then did a jerky dance with his entire body. His hands released from Conrad's throat. Conrad felt like all the blood rushed to his head at once. He coughed and gasped for air. Keyes and Fryer helped Conrad off of his feet.

"You got some big ass balls," Fryer said to Conrad. "I'll give you that."

Keyes didn't agree. "No, the idiot has balls for brains. You don't piss Bavardi off. He's a psychopath. You don't cross someone you can't take in a fight. Nobody can take that psychopath."

Conrad couldn't help but ask, "Then why did ENTECH hire him if he's a psychopath?"

Amati was standing over Bavardi's twitching body. He clutched the Taser gun he used on Bavardi in his right hand in case the team member decided to get back up.

Amati turned around and faced Conrad.

"Why hire him? Because Bavardi's a tough son-of-a-bitch. If things get out of hand, Bavardi can take a bullet to the head and keep on coming. I just shocked him with enough voltage to take out three guys, and Bavardi's going to recover from that jolt in minutes. Now get your heads on straight. We can't fuck this job up. We do that, we're out of the business, and we're out for good. You're out, you're fucking dead. Got it, people? You'll count the money you made in the grave."

Bavardi got up off the ground.

He refused Amati's help.

"Bavardi," Amati said, "stop playing games. You can have all the fun you want when this is over. When you're on my time, you do as I fucking say, or next time, I don't get the Taser gun. I'll just shoot you between the eyes and call it a day. Better yet, the rest of us get the cut of your pay. You want that to happen?"

Bavardi gave Conrad a shifty-eyed glance. Satan had left his expression, and the stoic solider returned. "No, sir, I'm straight. I want my cut."

"Good, now move out."

Keyes had Conrad by the arms from behind, and Fryer stood in front of them, shielding the hostage from Bavardi who stayed with Amati at the very front of the pack.

Conrad wasn't sure where they were at this point. Thick woods surrounded them for miles. There was a dirt road Amati had traveled, and the van was tucked away off that road and well hidden. Now the group was taking a trail through the woods to an unknown destination. NO TRESPASSING signs appeared periodically during their journey nailed into the body of trees.

Where are they taking me, Conrad kept thinking.

"The area is under constant surveillance," Amati said, updating his crew. "If anybody stumbles on this land, they're either escorted off the property or shot on sight. I just got word from our superiors that Henry and his crew are close. That gives us roughly two hours to get ready. We make this quick. We don't give them time to think or strategize. It'll soon be dark, and we don't want the sun down when they show up. Darkness is not our friend."

Twenty more minutes of hiking on a trail, their destination appeared cut out of the woods. Conrad read the sign on the tall perimeter fence topped with reams of barbed wire mesh:

ENTECH INDUSTRIES
PRIVATE PROPERTY
TRESPASSERS WILL BE SHOT ON SIGHT

A gated entrance opened up. This looked like the outside of a prison, Conrad thought. A military jeep with two armed guards pulled up and questioned Amati. After a short back and forth conversation, the team was allowed inside the secure area. The gate closed behind them.

Up ahead, Conrad couldn't believe what he was seeing.

Things were only getting worse.

Chapter Nine

Conrad studied the oversized helicopter. He imagined soldiers spilling out of it in wartime situations. The helicopter was black and menacing. Conrad had no idea where they were going in the bird. The private landing pad was suspicious. He thought back to ENTECH INDUSTRIES. Conrad figured ENTECH didn't sell children's toys.

The buildings surrounding the air pad were mostly offices and two story buildings with black tempered glass windows.

ENTECH remained a mystery.

Armed guards started to appear from many of the buildings. Like Amati's team, they were on edge. They expected Conrad's father to come in with gun's blazing.

The group approached the helicopter.

"There's our ride," Amati told everybody. "There's already a pilot waiting inside the Mi-17. That'll take us to where we're going. We wait for Henry and his team to show up. They'll check them in at the gates, they hop on board our ride, and we stay with Conrad. Nothing will happen to us as long as we've got a gun on Conrad."

Fryer stepped in first to take the job before Bavardi could. "I'll keep on a gun on him, sir."

"Okay, Fryer, but I want two guns on him. Keyes, you back Fryer up. Now let's wait in the chopper. It won't be much longer that we're airborne. Once we deliver Henry and his team to their destination, get ready for your paychecks. They're going to be big. First round of drinks are on me."

Keyes and Fryer helped Conrad into the Mi-17. They strapped him into one of the seats and secured him. Their nozzles stayed pointed in Conrad's direction.

Time dragged on, and Keyes gave Conrad a once over. "I always wanted to know what Henry Garfield's other son was like. You're nothing like Duke."

"He's got Garfield in him somewhere," Fryer said. "I don't know of any son-of-a-bitch with the stones to head butt Bavardi in the face like that."

"Balls for brains," Keyes said. "That's all it is with all you men. I have a feeling we're going to be at a standstill for awhile. I'd be curious to see what's going on in that installation we're flying to. "Private research" is a pretty vague. I still feel bad for double crossing Henry. We've worked for him for so long."

"Doesn't matter what kind of work our bosses do. It's about money, not loyalty," Fryer said. "Henry trained us, sure. He gave me an opportunity to work after my time in the service was up. Henry's a good man, yeah, but business is business. He's getting older too. You don't retire from this job. You either quit or die. I'm learning my lesson from this situation. After this job, I'm quitting the business. I'll take my chunk of money, lay low, and then meet a nice woman, have her pop out a few kids, get a cushy safe job, and do whatever I want for the rest of my life."

Keyes disagreed with that ideology. "I still feel bad for screwing over my mentor."

"No, ENTECH screwed him over," Fryer said. "They planned this whole expedition. There's no loyalty in the business. How's that your fault? It's not."

Amati told them all to shut up. "Not another word about the mission. You keep your ears open."

Amati was called on his walkie. His face lit up.

"What is it, boss?" Bavardi asked.

"Henry's team is here. They checked in at the front gates. They're unarmed, and they're coming willingly."

Everybody tensed up. Conrad peered out of the side door of the Mi-17. A large group of armed guards was escorting Henry, Duke, and two other persons he didn't know to the chopper. The team was dressed in black military garb.

Conrad tried to read his father's face, but it didn't betray any emotion. Duke, on the hand, looked like he wanted to start cracking skulls. The other soldiers, a man and a woman, shared the same intense expression as Duke.

Amati met up with Henry before they got too close to the Mi-17.

Henry started talking first. "What is this all about? I've known you for how many years, and you're pulling this shit, Amati? It starts with you, but it doesn't stop with you. After you showed me those horrible pictures of my son assaulted, I dialed up ENTECH. My contact's not answering his phone. ENTECH could be compromised. Even if they weren't, why are they having you kidnap my son and having us go through all of this bullshit? Another thought, why would you agree to do any of this, Amati, at any price?"

Without warning, Henry rolled on the ground, tripped up Bavardi, and landed four direct blows to Bavardi's skull. "I know it was you who hurt my son!"

Henry stomped on Bavardi's stomach. Bavardi was about to get back up when Amati stepped between them. Bavardi was snarling, and Henry was eyeing the blood on his hands with pleasure.

Keyes and Fryer both aimed their weapons at Henry. Amati showed Bavardi his stun gun. "Calm the fuck down, everybody."

Bavardi's face demanded violence. Then as quickly as he got worked up, Bavardi was calm again.

"This isn't a time for questions or explanations," Amati said. "Your team is getting on that chopper. We're all going to our destination. That's it. Nothing else needs to be discussed."

"You're wrong. A lot needs to be discussed. How much did they offer you?" Henry laughed at his own question. "I bet it was a ridiculous number, perhaps in the millions? Sure, they can offer any sum if they're not planning to pay you. I'm telling you, we all work for the same company, and they're trying to pull a fast one on all us. If you'd just take a moment to think. I can't reach my trusted contact at ENTECH. There's something wrong here."

"I'm smart enough to handle myself," Amati argued. "Just because you trained me and hired me doesn't mean I have to answer to you for the rest of my life. I'm done with this business. This is my final job. I've had too many close calls in the line of duty. I'm almost as old as you are, Henry, and I'm damn sick of this shit."

"So you're going soft on me?" Henry scoffed. "There's no convincing you to think rationally. Fine. You've got my son. What's the mission? What hell are you throwing us into?"

"That's none of your concern until we get there," Amati said. He snapped his fingers, and the armed guards from the base urged Henry's team into the chopper. "Now get in the helicopter. If you do anything, my boys will kill your son."

The mention of his son changed Henry's temperament. "We're going along with your plan. We're unarmed. ENTECH's goons checked us over real good. It might as well have been a prostate exam. They didn't get their gloves dirty, because we're clean."

Henry's team followed his lead as he entered the helicopter. When Conrad met his father's eyes, he could see through the man's steel facade.

"I'm so sorry, son," Henry said. "You never should've been involved. Forgive me."

Duke gave Conrad a smile and whispered in that brotherly way, "*Don't worry, pussy. We've got a plan. You'll be back at your apartment crying into a pillow and reading books in no time.*"

Bavardi and Amati were the last to get into the chopper. Amati sat next to the pilot.

"Strap yourselves in tight," Amati said. "We're going into the hot zone."

Chapter Ten

A half hour into the helicopter ride, Henry introduced his team to Conrad.

"Everybody, this is my son, Conrad."

Henry pointed to the woman with no shirtsleeves, showing off her bronzed and toned arms. She had a buzz cut and strong hazel eyes.

"This is Scoop. We call her scoop because she used to be a field reporter, until she put down the pen, picked up a gun, and joined the service. She made the right choice. Scoop's a helluva a good solider."

Scoop gave Conrad a good once over. "So Duke told me you lost your balls? Let's hope we can find them again. Maybe when this is over, I can help you. Duke never told me how handsome you are."

Conrad swallowed hard. He was about to come back with something when Henry pointed at the other solider, a softer looking version of Bavardi. He imagined Sylvester Stallone meets *Tiger Beat* magazine.

"This is Dirty Poncho," Henry said. "He never leaves a mission without being covered in some kind of crazy shit. Blood, mud, gunpowder, ash, you name it, he'll be caked in it by the time this is over."

Dirty Poncho's eyes wouldn't leave Bavardi, Fryer, and Keyes. When they did for a split second, he winked at Conrad.

Henry asked, "Are you okay, Conrad?"

"I feel like hell, but my head's not ringing as hard as it did earlier. I'll live. *Maybe*."

"I'm so sorry this is happening," Henry said to Conrad. "You deserve a better explanation about what we do. I recruit people to work for ENTECH. We call these people Post-Service Operatives.

The PSO's are mostly ex-military, retired soldiers, or good ol' boys who can serve their country better through private means. I'm a talent scout, and I also go on missions. ENTECH takes on anything from terrorism, drug runners, meth cookers, hostage situations, and foreign matters against the United States. We could be in Istanbul one week, and a month later, we're in Missouri kicking in the door of a child pornography ring.

"We're America's shovel. We dig up the shit that the government is too busy to handle, and we bury it deep into the ground. It's not exactly legal, but the crime we're fighting requires that special touch. There's hundreds of us involved in this line of work. It's a special calling. The only problem, it appears our company has been compromised. These idiots think they're getting paid to take us somewhere, and that's it, easy and done. I'm not sure what's going to happen, but I do know it's not what Amati and these bozos have in mind. We're going to do everything to keep you safe until the shit at ENTECH blows over. Until then, I want to find out what this mission is. It might tell us what's going on at ENTECH."

Conrad had no idea what to say to everything that his father told him. It didn't make him feel any better that they were flying over an ocean. There wasn't land in any direction. They were flying over the Gulf of Mexico and going God knows where.

Amati spoke into the loudspeaker. His voice was sharp with authority. "We're approaching the hot zone, so shut the fuck up back there. Any minute, we're touching down."

Chapter Eleven

Conrad wasn't sure what Amati meant by "hot zone". He imagined trench warfare, bombs bursting, and one large number of soldiers shooting at another set of soldiers. For a hot zone, the area was quiet. There was only ocean and the horizon line that was reducing itself from a red-orange color to an early evening purple.

Ten more minutes passed with agonizing sluggishness. Everybody in the helicopter, including Amati's men, was getting antsy. Only a sliver of daylight remained to paint their destination, which was a huge shape in the shadows. It was a long platform with legs that lifted it hundreds of feet above the ocean. He thought of an oil platform, except this was so big, he imagined four platforms combined.

This wasn't an offshore oil drilling rig.

Conrad knew it in his guts.

Large lights gave shape to the platform. Single level and multiple level buildings stood on the platform. The place had no identity or obvious purpose. The pilot was angling in for a landing on the helipad. When he touched down, Amati sounded distressed.

"Okay, team, move out. I don't know how long we're waiting for these late fuckers, but the plan's the same. Move everybody out to the platform, but first, have them dig out the supplies from the helicopter's bottom compartments.

Conrad was escorted out of the helicopter by Bavardi this time. The man twisted his arm hard behind his back, and Conrad gave a pained gasp, but nobody could hear him as the helicopter's propellers kept chopping at air. Bavardi directed Conrad across the helipad at gunpoint to a large door that was the size of a warehouse entrance. Sensor lights came on to bathe the way in blue-white. Fryer and Keyes had his father's team at gunpoint.

Henry and Duke were hauling what looked like a large steel toolbox. Scoop and Dirty Poncho were carrying one just like it too.

"What's in the box?" Henry asked. "It's goddamn heavy."

Amati arrived last and didn't answer the question. The man was too busy searching the open platform.

"What's going on here, Amati?" Henry demanded. "Is something *wrong*? You didn't think this through. Who assigned you this mission? Are you sure, they're from ENTECH? You're too busy thinking dollars and not logistics. You wonder why you never were promoted to my position, Amati? You're impulsive. These jobs require people putting their lives on the line. Critical thinking is everything. The burden is heavy. It's one you can't shoulder, asshole."

Amati erupted, "Say another word, I shoot your son myself!"

Keyes spoke. "Where's the other chopper? You said somebody would be here to take us away, and what about our money?"

Fryer was next with his concerns. "You said this would go smoothly, Amati. Did you fuck us?"

Bavardi growled under his breath and tensed Conrad's arm harder behind his back. Conrad feared the man would rip his arm off if the plan went south. After head butting the bastard, Bavardi would kill Conrad for free.

"They're just late," Amati kept saying, "or we're early. That has to be it. Everything's fine."

Amati checked his watch and kept checking it.

The tension was thickening. The longer it was silent, Conrad thought somebody would talk, but they didn't. Conrad's eyes couldn't adjust to the darkness out there in the ocean. It was dark and mysterious, and it would remain that way.

From up in the sky, two great yellow eyes flashed. A helicopter hovered over the platform. It was hard to see in the dark. Conrad was half-blinded by the intense orbs of light. He could see the two machine gun turrets armed on the sides of the helicopter.

Amati was relieved. "See, I told you ENTECH was on schedule. We'll be out of here in no time. First round of drinks are on me, like I said earlier."

Everything happened so fast. Bullets were spit from the sky. The death rain pinged hard against steel, shedding bright orange sparks. Both teams fell back towards the building closest to the helipad. Conrad was used as a shield to protect Bavardi. Hundreds of rounds were unleashed from the twin turret machine guns. The assault was deafening. Conrad saw the entrance to the main building start to open like a garage door. Once it was open, the bullet fire increased. Bullets rained down in a death wall, pushing them towards the door. They were forced to retreat inside. The moment everybody was inside, the entrance closed itself.

The bullets had ceased, but not the action. Bavardi had lost his firearm while running for his life. Bavardi grabbed Conrad and tried to force him into a headlock. Before that happened, Bavardi was attacked from behind. Conrad heard that wicked snap crunch of knuckles against jawbone. Bavardi was taken down by Henry. Bavardi clutched onto his mouth as blood funneled through his hands. Did he spit out teeth? No time to know really, Conrad stayed down and watched the action unfold.

Scoop got herself into high gear. She scissor kicked Keyes across the room into a wall. Dirty Poncho made short work of Fryer, giving him a solid blow to the solar plexus with two fists, and then elbowing him right in the nose. Blood shot out Fryer's nose. Next, Henry had Amati up against the wall with his arm twisted behind his back. Duke was collecting the guns taken from the other team members and handing them to Dirty Poncho and Scoop.

Henry ordered everybody to keep Amati's team covered. Conrad watched his dad shove Amati up against a steel wall two more times. "Now what the fuck is this all about?" Amati couldn't restrain the panic from his voice. "Look, I don't know! I don't know! This wasn't supposed to happen like it did. I was paid to do as I was told. This was not how it was supposed to go down."

"Who gave you this job?"

"ENTECH. I told you."

"If that's true, then when did ENTECH give you this mission?"

"It was only days ago. This was a rushed job."

"Why didn't they just hire us for a job? Why all the hoops to jump through? Why involve Conrad?"

Amati was flustered. Henry kept twisting his arm, and the man caved against the pain. "This isn't like the other jobs. They were afraid you'd say no, and they needed someone of your expertise fast. This is an escalating situation. That's what they told me."

"What is this place?"

"That I don't know."

Henry twisted Amati's arm even more. "Liar! I hope they paid you a mint, because I'm going to beat your fucking face into raw dog meat. Then maybe if I'm nice, I'll drive a bullet through the back of your head and throw you off the edge of the platform."

"No, wait!" Amati shouted. "Release my arm, please. I'll tell you everything I know. I double crossed you, but that doesn't matter, because they double crossed me too."

"You fuck me in my ass, and now your ass is getting fucked. Hurts, doesn't it? How far back do we go, Amati? We've been Post-Service Operatives for how long? We're supposed to serve our country, not ourselves. Then you have the gall to include my son in this mess? So tell me what you know, everything. Tell me a good story, dick face."

Henry released Amati's arm. He aimed a Desert Eagle pistol right at Amati's face, the very gun Henry had taken from Amati when they'd started running from the chopper's gunfire.

"Look in this room," Amati said. "This is the only secure quadrant in the building."

Everybody was sizing up the room now. It was a simple steel square with an exit leading back to the helipad and another set of double doors leading deeper into the installation. Both doors had a light bulb above them that glowed bright red. There were shelves of food supplies, medical supplies, and large quantities of bottled water. By the exit door were the two steel boxes Henry's team had carried in from the helicopter.

Nobody knew what was inside those boxes.

Amati was pouring sweat. He pointed at the steel boxes. "All I had to do was deliver your team here, Henry, along with those supplies. I was to leave on that chopper until it opened fire on us. You know the rest. Everything's fucked."

"So what is this place?" Henry asked.

"It's a research facility."

"So we're here to destroy whatever's in this building?"

"I think so. I wasn't told directly. At first, I thought this was a search and rescue mission. Then I was told that the original project taking place here was scrapped. This is no longer a research facility for environment affairs. It's a chamber of horrors. They want everything in this place destroyed. Then the scientists could come here, see what went wrong, and start over."

"Then why not blow this place off the map?" Henry asked. "Napalm the shit out of this steel box and call it a day, right? They could start over, no problem."

"They're afraid whatever's in here could fall into the water beneath our feet. If that happens, it'll spread, and then containing it would be impossible."

"What   will   spread?"

"Listen to me, this is more important. They said ENTECH hired twelve other squads to clean up this mess. Every squad's been taken out, no survivors each time. They asked me to kidnap Conrad to guarantee your help. ENTECH is desperate. They didn't want to take the chance that you'd say no. And you're one of the best, Henry."

"What does ENTECH want us to destroy?"

"*Lampreys*."

"Lampreys?"

Amati was in his own head. "I should've known better. You're all good people, and I betrayed you, but you don't understand. I was recently diagnosed with pancreatic cancer. The doctor said I have six months to a year before I succumb to the illness. I just wanted to live high for a while before I died. With the money they were going to pay me, oh man, I'd go out like a fucking fiesta.

"Look, we're here now without a choice in the matter and I'm willing to help. We can clean this situation up. Let's band together and kick some ass like the good old days. ENTECH had a good argument. If we can't stop what's on this installation, nobody can. That could mean death for everybody. If this spreads, there's no stopping it. The lampreys are out of control. I've seen pictures and security feeds. They're an abomination. Somebody has to stop them, and the only person is you, Henry."

Bavardi dug into his belt and pulled out a snub-nosed bulldog. Amati's forehead bloomed red. Amati's eyes were wild, frozen in that death stare, as his body lost its balance and fell backwards. The dead man landed in his own scattered brains. By the time everybody reacted to Amati's execution, Bavardi already had his gun aimed at Conrad's head.

Everybody aimed their guns at Bavardi, including Henry. "Put the gun down, Bavardi. Can't you see this isn't going to work out in your favor?"

Bavardi face wasn't intimidating anymore. He was terrified. "I shot Amati, so I'll shoot this maggot too. I'm not going into that place. You go in, and I'll wait here. Conrad won't get hurt if you complete the mission. Fuck Amati, fuck ENTECH, and fuck you guys. I'm taking Conrad with me as collateral. You get him back alive if you kill everything in there and survive. ENTECH told me if Amati caved, I could take over. My job's to ensure you go in there and clean house."

Everybody was startled when the exit to the platform opened. Bavardi looked around in confusion. Then it occurred to him somebody was listening. There were security cameras everywhere.

A deep voice spoke on the intercom. *"Step outside while the others complete the mission."*

Conrad was forced to backpedal with Bavardi as they retreated onto the platform. Conrad watched his father and brother and their looks of horror and helplessness. Then the garage closed again. He was all alone with Bavardi.

Chapter Twelve

Henry ran to the exit door. There wasn't any mechanism to open or close it. Conrad couldn't be reached. Whoever had closed it, it had been done by a remote signal. Amati had created so many problems in so little time. Amati felt remorse for what he'd done to the team. Faced with cancer, he had made poor decisions, but Henry wasn't Amati. Faced with death, Henry had to make the correct, critical decisions to save everybody and somehow get Conrad back from Bavardi.

Bavardi, now there was a beast of a problem. Bavardi was a good solider, but he'd also suffered a good deal of psychological torture in his time. He was captured by a rogue group of terrorists in Iraq. He was taken to the bottommost dwelling of a cave and tortured for two months straight. Bavardi survived, having escaped his cell and killing everybody involved with his bare hands. Henry hired him because of his heroism, but he also required the man to take medication and visit a therapist. Bavardi suffered from violent tendencies. And *that* man had his son. Henry was scared to think what Bavardi could do to his son if he had the chance. Conrad had no fighting skills. He was a college English professor. This was not a good place for him.

Henry put that information aside. First, he had to find out what Keyes and Fryer knew about Amati's workings with ENTECH and what was going on inside these buildings.

Duke, Scoop, and Dirty Poncho had each of them at gunpoint.

"Tell me what you know, Fryer," Henry said. "Go."

Before anything could be said, the intercom addressed them, "FIVE MINUTES BEFORE ENTRY."

"Shouldn't we find out what's in those boxes," Fryer argued. He kept eying the barrel of Duke's pistol. "Look, Keyes and I are as confused as you are. Amati said we'd take you guys here, drop you off, and we'd get paid two million a piece. None of this other shit was supposed to happen. Everybody's ass got fucked on the deal."

Keyes was angry, and she didn't lose an ounce of nerve with a gun in her face. "Yes, we betrayed you, but we're in here together now. I'm assuming whatever's behind that door is pretty fucking scary. I know nothing you don't already know."

"FOUR MINUTES BEFORE ENTRY."

Henry did his best to keep his head on straight. Too many concerns and ideas were attacking him at once. "Duke, find out what's in those boxes. Dirty Poncho, keep your guns on these two. I need to think."

ENTECH was more solid and trustworthy than the United States government. So what had happened? Why did ENTECH set up the kidnapping?

Confusion.

Everything was so mixed up.

Soldiers, good, honest Americans, had turned against him. This was by design. Amati was coming back to himself before Bavardi shot him in the head. The group that perpetrated this mission was smart and deceptive.

Henry had to be smarter than ENTECH.

He also had to be safe.

"We're working together," Henry said, making his decision. "Take your guns off of Fryer and Keyes. We have to get along if we're going to live."

"Are you sure?" Duke was eying his fellow comrades like dog shit. "They betrayed us."

"Yes, I'm sure. Lower your weapons. Now open those boxes."

"TWO MINUTES BEFORE ENTRY."

Duke did as his father told him.

Everybody's jaw dropped.

Henry smiled. "So everybody else failed to complete their mission in this place, huh? At least it looks like we have a fighting chance now. *Let's go tear this place a new one.*"

Chapter Thirteen

When the giant door leading into the installation closed behind them, Conrad was shoved onto the ground by a snarling Bavardi. The lights on the platform were all on, painting everything in blue-white. It was storming hard, and Conrad was drenched and cold to the bone. The helicopter that had opened fire on them had touched down next to the Mi-17.

"On your knees, NOW!" Bavardi barked. "You know how long it takes to beat a man to death? You're going to find out, Conrad. I still owe you from earlier."

Conrad pointed at the helicopter. What he saw was grotesque. "Look!"

Conrad was kicked on the side of the head. What he saw in the helicopter vanished from his registry. He rolled sideways, blinking the stars from his eyes. He had to keep his eyes shut, because the white hot flashes of pain were so intense. That would make two instances of severe head trauma in a short period of time. Conrad clutched his hands with both hands.

Bavardi shouted, "*No, no, no, this can't be happening!*"

Conrad had seen the blood caking the inside windows of the helicopter. The shells of two ravaged bodies were slumped over in their seats. They looked like red smears through the screen of hard pounding rain. The details didn't matter. The end result was the same. Both pilots were dead.

Bavardi opened one of the doors, shoved aside one of the bodies, and tried to use the radio. "Somebody's destroyed the radio." Bavardi was overwhelmed. "Whatever got to them will try to get to us next. Jesus Christ, what is happening here? Those bodies were...*eaten.* Just like Amati."

Conrad wasn't sure what to do now. He stayed on the ground waiting for the aching swell in his head to subside so he could think clearly. Bavardi kept whispering flustered nonsense under his breath and pacing the platform. The main thing Conrad heard was, "*I'm not getting eaten. Fuck a bunch of that.*"

Conrad stayed quiet. He didn't want Bavardi to come out of his head. The man might remember how he wanted to beat Conrad to death. The problem, Conrad couldn't stay quiet. From behind the chopper, from out of the shadows, someone was creeping up behind Bavardi.

Chapter Fourteen

Weapons galore!

Henry and his newly formed team basked in the array of arms. Six Gatling guns, a case of hand grenades, and enough ammunition to miss a hundred times and still kill something comprised the arsenal.

"ONE MINUTE UNTIL ENTRY."

Henry had to strategize, and quick. "Arm yourselves. Take what you can carry. We're not sure what we're up against here. We stay together as a unit. Just like our other missions."

Before Henry could finalize a plan, there was a banging sound coming from the ceiling. Henry could see the ceiling cave in and dent outwards. Whatever was coming, it was gigantic and powerful.

"Look!" Duke shouted. "What the hell is doing that? It has to be huge."

Amati's body lay there dead one second, the next, up from the floor, burst three dark black eel-like monsters that were twenty feet long. They had flat heads and circular sucker faces. Teeth jutted out in a circular fashion—and was it Henry's imagination, or were their teeth spinning in circular fashion too? Behind those teeth was a raw pink muscle bound throat ready to drag down the bits of whatever it consumed. He imagined the teeth to be motorized weapons. Each face dug into Amati's corpse, latched on, and sucked in deep. They dragged Amati's corpse through three separate holes in the floor after tearing his body into crude pieces. It happened in seconds.

Amati's body was gone.

Whatever was making the banging sounds at the ceiling had moved on.

"What the fuck was that?" Fryer said. "They were like snakes."

Henry remembered what Amati had said earlier about lampreys.

"Come on, we've seen worse before. We're trained for this."

"Have you seen worse than this before, Henry?" Keyes demanded. "I don't know what missions you've been on, but I've *never* seen anything like that. Shit! That was horrible."

Dirty Poncho and Scoop came out of their shock.

"Did you see those hideous teeth?" Dirty Poncho posed. "Teeth can't spin in place like that. They have meat grinder faces."

Henry had to calm his team. He had to calm himself too. "Like Amati said before he was executed, they're lampreys on million forms of chemicals and steroids. There's nothing natural about them."

"No wonder they want them killed by us," Scoop said. "If they blew this place up, who knows what might fall into the ocean and swim to land. Normal people would be defenseless. We'd be sushi to those things."

Duke was standing over the holes punched into the floor. "There's slime all over these holes. Nasty shit. I guess they can lubricate their own way. What I don't get is, if they're so strong, why haven't they escaped by now? They should be long gone."

The intercom crackled on. A disturbed man spoke, *"Because she's not ready to leave. She's needs her strength. Soon, we'll be ready to leave. We're all so very hungry, and you're on the menu. Come on in. The door's open. Let me be the first to welcome you inside."*

The entry door into the installation opened and stayed open.

The words repeated in Henry's mind. The way the voice spoke, the person sounded mentally unbalanced.

"Okay, it's time to show some balls," Henry said to everybody. "We've seen this kind of action before." He looked at Keyes. "Okay, not exactly. The same rules apply, though. Shoot to kill, being careful not to gun down any survivors. Whatever happened here, they might have some answers for us. You know what to do. Lug what you can carry, and let's move out. Different enemy, same end result. We live, they die. Now mother said to clean house before she gets home or we don't get any supper. Grab your guns and let's go kick some ass."

Chapter Fifteen

Bavardi gave a start when he too saw the man coming at him from behind. Conrad stayed back while Bavardi motioned to take the stranger down. The problem, the man's hand snapped off at the wrist when Bavardi grabbed it. Conrad's eyes tripled. Bavardi cowered backwards with disbelief playing in his wild eyes.

Conrad kept blinking rainwater from his eyes. The storm hadn't let up. The strange figure was a man with long and stringy white hair. He was wearing a bloody white lab coat. The man's face was gray as a mushroom and his eyes were deep dark wells in the sockets.

"You step any closer, I'll shoot you in the face." Bavardi had his pistol raised. "Now who are you? Identify yourself."

Bavardi saw the fresh blood dripping from the man's lab coat.

"You killed the pilots? Why did you do it? Don't you want off of this installation?"

"Of course I do, but only when her belly is full."

Bavardi gave Conrad a confounded stare. It was the first time he could view Bavardi as a human being and not a savage animal.

"You're obviously out of your mind right now. Tell me your name. Did one of those things get to you?"

"I'm Dr. Sutherland. This is my project. I thank you for your contribution to science ahead of time. Your body will digest quite well. She can handle just about anything, even a big man like yourself. Her hunger is voracious."

"Whose hunger?"

Dr. Sutherland raised the stump of his hand up to his face. He regarded it with little concern and much fascination. "I feel nothing, not a single bit of pain. They've given me such power. I'm her vessel. I exist only to serve her. I feed what needs to be fed, and right now, the hunger pains in Mama's belly are unbearable! Damn the hunger pains!"

The doctor bent in half, clutching his belly. His voice was stilted, doubling in power and verve. "SHE MUST FEED!"

Conrad watched in horror when the doctor's severed hand started to vibrate on the ground. The doctor picked up his hand, and out from the stump of his hand shot out dozens of worm-sized creatures. The worm creatures wove themselves together, and the hand reattached itself. Then the doctor wiggled his fingers.

"Look, his face!" Conrad watched the doctor's eyes roll into back of his head and tiny jagged teeth sprout from the edges of his sockets.

"Stand back!" Bavardi said, opening fire. He emptied the clip, and the shots tore through the man with no effect.

The doctor's transformation wasn't complete. The man opened his mouth wide. Conrad could hear the uncouth snap and dislocating of his jaw. The man's mouth doubled in size. The mouth formed a circular shape, and out from the soft stretched tissue sprouted those jagged triangular teeth. The teeth spun like a fan in a circular motion as did the teeth in the man's eyes.

"Run, Conrad! Find your father. Tell him I'm sorry for everything. This was a terrible mistake! We should never have come here!"

Conrad wasn't sure where to run. When he finally did decide, Bavardi howled in pain. Conrad wasn't sure what to make of what was transpiring. The sound of high winds, then that suction sound of an impossibly giant fan swishing through air, the skin on Bavardi's face twitched and was sucked outwards. Then in a ripping motion, squares and strands of meat from his face was torn and dragged into the three holes in the doctor's face. In seconds, Bavardi's face was almost stripped down to the skeleton, and the man was still screaming in pain.

The doctor lifted up his shirt with both hands. From the chest down to his navel writhed a giant circular mouth made of intestinal tissue. Around those pink visceral lips sprouted six inch teeth just like the ones at the doctor's mouth. A stronger current of suction ripped Bavardi's guts from out of his belly. Bavardi was forced into the high speed mouth-belly. Conrad retreated in horror.

The platform was covered in puddles of rainwater. He couldn't complete five steps without feeling like he was going to hit the deck. Conrad stopped, searching for an escape. He refused to turn around, hearing Bavardi's body being disembodied.

That was what the doctor was doing.

Devouring him.

Conrad knew he'd be next. There was no control panel to get back inside the installation where he'd last seen his father and brother. Would he dare to throw himself off the edge of the platform and plunge himself into certain death?

Drown or be dissected alive, which was better?

He chose neither.

Conrad spotted a ladder going up over the building and onto the roof. He raced to it, climbed its length, and crawled onto the roof. The installation went on and on from his vantage point. In pure darkness, he had no compass to decide his next move. He chose his steps carefully. There had to be an access down into the building somewhere. Conrad shivered in the cold rain. He was soaked through and through, but what chilled him more was watching Bavardi die.

Minutes passed, and the sound of rain pounding against him was drowned out when he felt that tugging sensation at his back. He lost his footing and tumbled to the ground. Conrad was being dragged by invisible hands. Pure force, pure suction, pure terror, Conrad released howls of alarm as he dug his fingers and feet into the ground, but he couldn't stop the momentum.

Conrad was headed straight for the doctor who had joined him on the roof.

Chapter Sixteen

Henry took the lead when guiding his well-armed team deeper into the installation. The door closed behind them after they each entered the next part of the building. No way out, Henry thought. They had no choice but to fight. The quicker they searched the place and wiped the place clean of the lampreys, the sooner he could search for Conrad. He prayed Bavardi didn't do anything to his son. Bavardi was sound of mind when he wanted to be, but otherwise...

They headed down a very long and narrow channel. Glass walls and class ceilings were everywhere. He imagined a high-end scientific lab of the future.

"This isn't what I expected," Henry said to his team. "There isn't a spot of blood anywhere."

Through many walls, they heard the hollow banging against steel. Walls were being punched through. There was also the uncouth sound of grinding bones.

Crickcrackcrickcrackcrickcrackcrickcrack.

The group heard a fierce yawp of pain.

"People are alive in this place," Duke said. "Or, they *were* alive."

"Keep moving." That was the best advice Henry could give his team. The hallway, the channel between two buildings, extended for what seemed like the length of a football field. When they approached another doorway, the coded key panel was turned inside as if someone had tried to lock in whatever was inside.

"Dirty Poncho, see what you can do to get us inside."

"You got it," Dirty Poncho said, putting down the heavy Gatling gun. "I'll have us inside in no time. Looks like someone did a rough job of disarming it. It won't take much to get it up and running again."

Henry pictured the creatures that ate Amati's body. This place had to be full of them. Would their weaponry be enough? He could fly them off of this rig if need be. As long as that Mi-17 was still parked on the platform, they had an exit strategy, but he wasn't leaving without Conrad.

Scoop kept eyeing Fryer and Keyes with disdain. Scoop hated the fact they had to work with people who essentially put them in this situation. Henry couldn't help but wonder what the other teams who'd died here had encountered.

Someone was sabotaging them from within, Henry knew. The voice over the intercom was a clue. It wouldn't only be the lampreys they would have to worry about. The odd assortment of weapons Amati's team had delivered here was also a concern. Gatling guns and grenades weren't typically used during ENTECH's missions. This wasn't a mission to better serve the country. This was somebody's operation. Somebody wanted them to carry around the hot shit guns for a reason.

"Got it ready to be opened, boss," Dirty Poncho reported. "Tell me when you're ready to go in."

Henry raised a fist in the air, clenched it, and then when he dropped his hand back down, Dirty Poncho engaged the door. It came open with a hermetic hiss. The way was dark inside. Henry was about to instruct his team to get out their flashlights when every light on the other side flickered on.

Now Henry knew someone was alive in this place working behind the scenes.

"Take universal precautions," Henry said. "I'll take point."

The heavy-duty lights saturated the hallways. There wasn't anything in the area but closed doors. Dirty Poncho tested a few of the locks. "These aren't on an electrical system. They're good old fashioned steel. Should I pick a door?"

"No, leave it." Henry wanted to stay quiet until he was sure they absolutely had to make noise. "Save your ammo. These lampreys aren't going to hide behind locked doors. I can't believe I'm saying this, but what we saw eat Amati was real. We didn't have a mass hallucination. This is something we've never been up against. When in doubt, pump it full of bullets until it's dead. This isn't a scientific exploration. This is a slaughter. Whether it's our slaughter or theirs is entirely up to you. Keep your heads on straight and your balls tight and we should make it out of here just fine."

They kept searching down a long stretch of hallways. There weren't any signs of violence or life. Fifty rooms later, they happened upon an elevator. It was stopped on their level. Everybody in the group except for Henry jumped when the elevator dinged and came open.

Duke ran to stop the elevator on their floor. Keyes, Fryer, and Scoop backed him up while Henry studied the six corpses occupying the inside of the elevator. Wild splashes of blood had congealed on the walls and floor. Henry imagined that these corpses had been stuffed into a microwave and cooked until they popped. Lab coated men and women were riddled with holes. He pictured lampreys the size of garden snakes boring tunnels into the bodies. The bodies were picked clean of seventy percent of their insides and muscle tissue.

Scoop noticed the female scientist's hands. Curled up like a claw, she had grabbed a lamprey in her dying moment and pulled into two halves. Both halves were rotting husks in her death grasp.

"Those teeth," Scoop said. "Christ, they're hideous. They latch onto you, slice into you with those gnarly teeth, and eat away. It's like a deli slicer on speed."

"I don't know a lot about lampreys," Keyes said, "but I took some science classes back in community college before I dropped out. We learned a little bit about these guys. Most lampreys aren't parasitic. They don't latch onto things and eat them to death. They don't have spinning teeth like that either. Nothing does. I saw what they did to Amati's body, goddamn blender-faces. They've been severely altered. I can only wonder what God-awful things these scientists are doing here to make them that way."

"Keep the elevator locked on this floor," Henry said. "I don't want anybody sneaking up on us that walk upright. Somebody is here, and they're either helping us or throwing us into harm's way, and I'm going to find out which."

The hallways were shaped in a square. The rooms were sealed off, but Henry wasn't so sure about busting down every door just yet. The building had three levels. They were on the bottommost level. Henry decided to take it floor by floor until they reached the top.

The group entered the elevator, doing their best to step around the corpses.

Dirty Poncho hit the button for level two.

Chapter Seventeen

What is with this guy?

Dr. Sutherland was a blur through the curtain of rain and darkness. Conrad could only see that giant sucker mouth gaping wide open as it sucked in more air to draw his helpless body into its deadly maw.

This time, the suction was much more powerful. The steel roof was denting and crumpling under the force.

Run you fucking idiot!

Conrad was an English Professor. He read books, drank expensive coffee, and read undergraduate papers. He didn't battle monsters!

He was winded after struggling on the ground for a minute. For Conrad to regain his energy to fight, it only took remembering Bavardi's guts unwinding from his body, and those guts spreading out across the platform and landing in a hungry mouth.

He got back up and ran for his life. Dr. Sutherland was a phantom in the darkness. He moved faster than Conrad did. He felt the air tug back his hair and shirt.

Soon, it would be flesh being tugged and torn.

"Stop running! I'm very hun-gry!"

There was a sonic boom. It was as if the doctor had saved up the strength for one great suck. A section of the roof was torn back like a tin can. The force of air had missed Conrad, and he thanked the ever-loving Lord that he was still wearing his skin.

The next problem, the roof wasn't secure. Parts of it started to crumble beneath his feet. He stepped into a hole. Conrad was pitched down into the darkness below. Conrad didn't touch down; he splashed down. He came awake swimming for his life in ice-cold water. Had he fallen off of the platform and into the ocean? It was impossible to know. There was only darkness and water.

Conrad thrashed his limbs and reached out for purchase of any kind. He swallowed a mouthful of nasty water. It wasn't salt water; it had a grainy texture and tasted like turpentine. Conrad was losing strength. He was dying in a cold and dark place alone. He imagined his father and his brother and how he'd never see them again.

Conrad couldn't fight for his life a moment longer.

His body failed him.

Conrad sank down into the dark abyss.

Chapter Eighteen

The elevator opened up to another narrow hallway. There was only one way to go, and that was forward. Henry led the team. Everybody was back-to-back so every angle was accounted for. They couldn't afford to be flanked by any enemy, human or lamprey. If there was one break in the chain, they would be crippled. Half the lights in the ceiling were broken. The ones that did shed light were few and far between, leaving large patches of darkness. Henry didn't need every inch of the place illuminated to see the pools of blood on the floor. Wild splashes covered the walls. Every red puddle was congealed and curdled. The victims had died days, if not weeks, ago. There wasn't a single corpse on the ground, except for the occasional random finger, hand, or torn off body part. Scattered about were items of clothing, mostly shoes, lab coats, torn fabric, and random articles.

Henry ordered for the group to stop.

"Listen," Henry whispered, "can you tell from how far out where that sound is coming from?"

Everybody tuned their ears to the faint sound. Something was crashing against metal. Steel was bending and warping under pressure. The noise was punctuated by the awful grating bone sound like from when Amati was being devoured earlier.

Crickcrackcrickcrackcrickcrackcrickcrackcrickcrackcrickcrac k.

"What the hell is that?" Fryer said. His eyes had doubled. "Look, I know I did wrong. I deserve to be here standing with you guys, but I don't want to be eaten like Amati. I mean, fuck that. Those things are clicking their teeth together. They're licking their chops. They're thinking about eating us, and it makes me sick."

Scoop scowled at him. She raised her Gatling gun. "You shove this down its throat and feed it a bullet supper. It'll win you a one-way ticket off the dinner menu. So shut up and stick a tampon in it before your pussy bleeds so hard your twat falls off. *Stupid bitch.*"

Keyes wasn't having it. "You say that shit to me again —"

Henry stepped between them. "We can't turn on each other. We'll deal with Fryer and Keyes later. Right now, we need them, and they need us, or we might as well all die like Amati. And you're forgetting, my son's out there with Bavardi."

Duke shared his father's concern. "My brother's a college professor. He's helpless out there. He'll die like everybody else on this installation if we don't hurry, and if Bavardi doesn't do something worse to Conrad than the lampreys first. So show some respect for our family and get over the situation and get your heads on straight."

That was enough motivation to get everybody back to the mission.

Henry guided everybody down the bloody hallway. Room doors started to appear marked by numbers. Many of the doors were either completely ripped from their hinges, punched into splinters, or riddled with gaping holes. Henry viewed the rooms long enough to understand the personal living quarters had been ransacked and those inside were murdered. The holes in the walls and doors varied from fist-sized, fingertip sized to sewer pipe thick.

Up ahead was a common area where several couches, a big screen television, and tables for a casual dining area were arranged. Henry imagined a college dorm setting. Scientists and workers congregated here during their social time. Now, the place was a bloodbath.

"Point your light at that television," Henry said to Keyes. "You see that?"

The large screen television had a lamprey stuck to the front. The teeth had latched in deep. The once slimy black body was now reduced to dried up beef jerky. Dirty Poncho made the connection before anybody else.

"I bet that television showed a person's face, and that lamprey went right for it, and it got electrocuted. The bastard didn't let go, even when its ass was being fried."

Keyes pointed at the floor. There was a limbless and headless human torso, and it was moving across the floor inch-by-inch. Sucking, slurping noises vibrated from the torso. "They're eating it from the inside out."

Henry could see the black bodies slithering within the torso. They had snaked through muscle tissue and flesh as their teeth spun like the blades of a bone saw and devoured their prey. What he didn't understand, the lampreys lower half stuck out of the body, and they were using their bodies to drag the torso to another location.

Henry asked, "Why didn't they just eat their kill and move on?"

"Disgusting! I don't care!" Keyes growled. "I'm going to blast it before it tries to eat me!"

Keyes unloaded eighty shots from the Gatling gun. The torso bounced as it took bullet after bullet. The lampreys that were within burst, each of them going up into mist. Their insides were like blackberry jelly.

"Fuck you," Keyes spat. "You're not eating me."

"They're not eating any of us," Fryer said, "but where are they? Why aren't they raining from the ceiling to get us?"

"That I don't know," Henry said. "It's all a guess. They'll show up eventually. You remember the way they burst from the ground to get Amati? They could be nearby and we wouldn't know it. That's why we've got to keep moving."

Henry kept imagining what Conrad would do up against a lamprey. It was a horrible thought he forced himself to avoid. Henry refused to believe his son was dead.

The team exited the living quarters. Only blood, clothing, and random pieces of the human bodies remained scattered. Whatever battle ensued, it appeared to be an ambush on a wide scale. The attack happened at once, not over an extended period of time.

Henry had a hard time accepting the idea the lampreys had formed a collective consciousness. Then again, he didn't know a damn thing about what was going on in this research installation. ENTECH was a prolific entity. Maybe government missions weren't all the company dealt with.

The hallway fed into a much larger room. There was a well-equipped kitchen and mess hall style seating. Henry imagined several hundred people could occupy the space at any given time. The tables were upended or in so many pieces. Blood colored everything. The ceilings were torn and gaping wide open. Whatever form of lamprey had attacked here, it was much bigger than the snake-sized ones. The Gatling gun in Henry's hands started to feel insignificant up against the strange enemy.

Henry couldn't see any of the posters or morale boosters on the walls of the dining area, they were so caked in gore. One sight made him pause. Bone shards from hundreds of bodies were embedded in the walls as if flung at many miles an hour.

Duke followed his father's stare. He used two fingers to pry a shard from the wall. "Damn. The piece of bone is in there good. You saw their teeth spin. I bet they chew them up, and then shit out the bones."

Scoop was searching the rest of the mess hall. She was walking across turned over chairs, broken pieces of table, and widening her stride to avoid the deeper puddles of blood. "Bone remains are here, and here...and here. I think Duke's right. They eat them up, and they shit them right out."

Keyes and Fryer were fixated on the ceiling. Keyes said, "There are bones and blood up in the duct systems too. It's as if these people were, I don't know, somehow sucked up into the ceiling, and this is what's left of the poor sons-of-bitches."

"We're not scientists," Henry said. "I don't care what they shit out. I only want them dead. Keep moving. Nothing here."

The team exited the cafeteria. They checked upstairs and located more living quarters that had been invaded. There were no survivors. Heading back down to the main floor, they located another narrow hallway that seemed to connect one building to another. The building they were about to enter had two steel double doors for an entrance. There was a sign marking the doors.

RESTRICTED AREA
LEVEL 4 CLEARANCE ONLY

Two checkpoint stations were set up to regulate access. Those stations were empty. The glass windows were shattered, the inside walls painted in blood. The team crossed through the checkpoints knowing it could be their blood shed next if they didn't watch out. When they were right up against the steel doors, Henry read a message painted in blood on the wall.

NOT SAFE INSIDE
KEEP LOCKED
DO NOT ENTER

The coded key panel was dismantled. The face was taken off, and the guts of circuits were hanging out. It was obvious that someone rigged the door to remain closed.

"Somebody has to be behind that door that knows what's going on," Henry said. "Dirty Poncho, work on that panel. We have to get inside. I don't care what that blood says."

Dirty Poncho put down his Gatling gun, unstrapped the travel tool kit strapped around his leg, and went to work on the door.

Chapter Nineteen

Conrad let his body go. He had nothing else left inside himself to fight. He would sink at the bottom of this unknown watery grave and never be found. If this mission was classified, friends and his old co-workers at Texas University would think Conrad killed himself because of Arielle. People would say he died of a broken heart and humiliation. He drank himself into suicide. The shocking truth of his death would remain untold. The downward spiraling of his life seemed so insignificant up against the threats on the installation. He'd seen more action in the past twelve hours than in his entire life, and now it was going to end on such a pathetic note.

This wouldn't be a peaceful death. The longer he went without air, his lungs painfully expanded in his chest. Almost two minutes under, his lungs felt like they would burst. Conrad thrashed his body, coming alive to save himself.

The pain overcame his weakness.

Anything for one precious gulp of air!

Then Conrad saw a hand reaching out to him. He couldn't see who it was in the dark depths of the strange waters. There was a faint bluish light above him that flickered on. Conrad stretched out his hand to grab hold of the lifeline. When he did, the hand didn't clasp onto him. It turned over, being a flimsy thing. The arm ended at the elbow. It had been crudely eaten at the stump.

Conrad unleashed a water-choked scream, "*Gaaaaaaaaaaaah*!"

There was a great swishing of water from beneath him. A wall of bubbles pounded into him. An invisible wave of motion worked like an undertow. He was sucked down and spun upside down. Forced down, he realized this would be his dying moment. Then suddenly the direction of the waves changed. Conrad was spit upwards. He was thrown above the surface. He struck a thick glass wall, and right next to him, was a metal ladder. Conrad clutched onto it for his life, gasping for air.

Conrad realized what he'd fallen into and he was terrified. This was an aquarium. He imagined the type used at Sea World. He had no idea how deep this aquarium was, but he sensed movement of something gargantuan below him.

Bobbing on the surface were random human appendages. They were mostly heads and hands. The bite marks on them were wild slashes and serrations. Those inflictions had caused decapitations and mutilations. Brown foam crowded each side of the tank. A vile mixture of deflated eyeballs, fingers, and chunks of faded intestines the color of hotdogs was mixed in that foam.

When Conrad put everything together, he climbed up the ladder quickly. The foam, the random pieces, it was all shit out of great monster's ass.

Conrad crawled onto a steel platform. He moved to get as far from the water's edge as possible. Every part of his body was exhausted from running from that crazy scientist on the roof. He could see the small gaping hole in the roof above. Rainwater was trickling down from outside. He was up at least three stories high, maybe more. Stairs channeled down the side of the aquarium. A man in a lab coat stood at the head of the stairway. He was clutching onto the rail for support with one hand, the other holding a bleeding wound on his side. The scientist wore an intense haggard expression of weariness and disappointment.

"You're lucky you escaped like you did," the stranger said with little conviction. "She must be saving her strength, because she normally would've sucked you right down and chewed your ass up. If she's saving her strength, she must be close to ready."

"Ready for what? How do you know so much?"

"I'll tell you everything when we get down from here. I get nervous standing up here. She's unpredictable."

"She, who?"

"Mama."

The scientist cut Conrad off before he could say anything else.

"Hold on with the questions, just follow me. There isn't much time before everything goes to hell. We both deserve a moment of peace before we die."

Chapter Twenty

Dirty Poncho was talking about a hermaphrodite hooker who charged double the going rate down in Mexico as he was tinkering with the key panel to get to the other side of the restricted area. He twisted wires and rebuilt destroyed connections, all the while trying not to fry himself. While Dirty Poncho was sharing yet another version of how he got his special nickname, Henry asked Fryer and Keyes questions.

"This place still has electricity, which is odd," Henry said. "How long has this place been out of commission, you think?"

Fryer shook his head. "Man, I wish I knew. Amati hired me and said all I had to was help transport Conrad. We get here, leave, and bam, a paycheck. I didn't get any of the details about the place itself."

"And bam, you're a piece of shit," Scoop said. "Wham, bam, go fuck yourself in your own ass."

Keyes aimed her Gatling gun at Scoop's midsection. "Keep talking shit, bitch."

Scoop grabbed the barrels and pointed them at the floor. "I'll take you in a fist fight any time. I don't need guns to back up my shit. You apparently do, Keyes."

Fryer stepped between them. "Stop it and hear me out. Amati did tell me one thing. It kind of slipped out while we were on the mission. ENTECH's been recording teams like us while they're clean-sweeping the installation. They wanted to see this project reach its full potential. I guess every group before us was a test run for data and analysis. Data for what, who knows? My guess, it's to see what these killing machines can do against trained forces.

"Amati said you and your team, Henry, were going to be the last resort before they did blow this place up with chemical weapons. The problem, and Amati said this himself, if any of the things fall into the ocean, there's a chance they can make it to land. If they find a populated area, it'll spread. We can't fail."

Keyes was furious. "You knew all of this, and you're just now talking about it?"

"I'm scared is all," Fryer admitted. "After seeing the number of dead bodies, I don't know how we're going to stop them. They're so many of those things. I thought this would be a straightforward search and destroy mission. I guess it's more involved than that."

"We'll figure out a way to fix this mess," Henry said. "First things first, we have to survey the area. Even more is on the line now. We're not just fighting for our lives. We're doing this for the lives of innocent people. We're in the Gulf of Mexico. It's not that far of a swim for a creature equipped for those kinds of conditions. If those people that hired Amati would've just talked to me instead of forcing us here, we could've mapped out a better strategy. But then again, it sounds like the people running the show doesn't care, or their heads are too far up their asses to catch a breath of air. They'll kill as many of us to ensure this private research doesn't go public. We still don't know everything about this place and the reasons we're here."

Scoop was more curious about the lampreys. "So why enhance the lamprey? I've done investigative journalism for years, and this installation doesn't make sense. It could be a terrorist weapon, *maybe*, but lampreys need water and moist conditions to survive. And outside of water, they don't travel well for too long. It'd be easier to create a super nuke rather than mutate a species of lamprey. There were hundreds of people working on this thing. I can only image the cost of this project. So why lampreys?"

A demented voice boomed over the intercom, giving everybody a jolt.

"YOU HAVE NO CONCEPT OF WHAT YOU'RE UP AGAINST. SHE WAS BORN HUNGRY AND SHE WILL DIE HUNGRY. ALL WE WANT TO DO IS DEVOUR YOU. WE'LL EAT AT YOUR SOFT MEAT AND SUCK THE MARROW FROM YOUR BONES. YOUR INSIDES ARE SO JUICY AND SO SWEET. TASTY SWEET MEAT IS ALL WE

WANT. MY STOMACH IS GROWLING JUST WATCHING YOU IN THE SECURITY CAMERA FEED. BUT NO HUNGER CAN MATCH MAMA'S HUNGER.

"GO AHEAD AND TRY TO STOP HER. THE ONES WHO CAME BEFORE YOU HAD BIG ARTILLERY JUST LIKE YOU. IT'LL DO YOU NO GOOD. SHE'S SO CLOSE TO BEING READY. SOON, VERY SOON, THIS PLACE WILL BE AN ABANDONED POST. YOU WILL ALL BE DEAD. THIS IS ONLY THE BEGINNING. WE WILL CHEW YOU UP AND SHIT YOU OUT. SO GO AHEAD. COME ON INSIDE. I'LL OPEN THE DOORS. BE MY GUESTS. I EXTEND A HEARTY INVITATION. COME IN AND DIE!"

Dirty Poncho dropped his tools when the key panel shot out a furious ball of sparks. The steel double doors opened. Everybody took several steps back. Every Gatling gun was aimed ahead of them. The room was impossible to navigate because the area was draped in pitch-black darkness.

"IT'S A SHAME. THESE CREATURES ARE SO BEAUTIFUL. I DESIGNED THEM MYSELF. YOU'LL BE THE FIRST TO DO BATTLE WITH THEM. I'LL WARN YOU. THEY'RE STARVING!!!"

Before Henry could direct his team, the demented voice added, "OH, YES, OF COURSE! THEY WANT TO SEE WHAT'S ON THEIR PLATES. LET ME LIGHT THE WAY!"

Every light flickered on in the expansive room. They couldn't see to the very back, the corridor was so long. Shattered glass covered the floor in glittery fragments. Cages, holding tanks, and aquariums to house large aquatic life had all been shattered. Everything in captivity had escaped, and the massive horde was charging right towards Henry and his team.

Chapter Twenty-Two

The storm outside had downgraded itself into a cool misting. The sky was pure darkness. The black didn't let up to give any dimension. His body was ice cold, but Bavardi didn't have feelings of any kind. He should be dead. He *was* dead. Only forty-percent of his body remained intact, as the rest had been devoured by Dr. Sutherland. Bavardi was only a vessel of brain function.

No pain, he kept thinking. *No pain. No pain at all.*

And thank God for the favor, he thought.

Bavardi was sprawled out on the helipad. There was hearing in his left ear, but in the right, he was deaf as a post. He heard the sound of rubber squeaking. Through his left eye, a lamprey had slithered into his socket, crawled through his broken sinus cavity, and channeled itself down his throat and into his belly. He sensed a colony of smaller lampreys burrowing into his intestines. What skin remained on his body, the monsters used to stay moist.

I am their vessel, Bavardi thought without knowing why. *I am nothing but meat to be eaten. I am a host. Use me as you will.*

The broken connections of his kneecaps and hipbones were reconnected. Bone and muscle were crudely fastened together. Bavardi saw the lampreys swim across the platform in a mass, using their thin leathery dorsal fins to propel them forward. The spinning of their teeth, like a motor fan, propelled them forward at impossible speeds. Easily, a hundred lampreys the size of snakes was burrowing into Bavardi's body. Serrated, chewed meat was squished together. Broken bones were fastened by lamprey bodies working in tandem to put back together a broken man. A stirring in his brain, he sensed lampreys crawl into his skull through his ear holes. The bastards were nesting in his brain. Their suction mouths dug into the hemispheres of his brain, as if plugging in.

Bavardi was theirs to use. Six lampreys combined to shape a crude bicep. Sucker faces doubled as hands and fingers. Bavardi was a walking monstrosity.

Mostly monster, very little human, Bavardi did what he could to hold on to the little part of himself that still existed.

I am a vessel.

No pain.

No pain at all.

Use me as you will.

Bavardi climbed the ladder leading to the rooftop. He didn't move in the direction Conrad had earlier when running from Dr. Sutherland. Bavardi hobbled across one building to another. He had no idea where he was going, but the lampreys did. They had a job to do and Bavardi had no choice but to help.

Chapter Twenty-Three

Conrad followed the mysterious man in the lab coat down the long stairway. Below the aquarium, there was a landing where several tables were covered in various papers, strewn files, and laptop computers. Dry erase boards were covered in drawings of the snake-eel creatures called lampreys. Mathematical equations, scientific jargon, and wild arrows pointing to the various parts of the lamprey covered most the board. The doctor, clutching his bleeding side, sat down on one of the chairs clumsily, and drank straight from a bottle of whiskey. The first pull wasn't enough, so he sucked down another. The guy's lab coat was soaked in a widening pool of blood. The injury was taking its toll on the man. What injury was a question Conrad wasn't quite ready to ask. The man seemed infirm and kept whispering and muttering things to himself.

"You should take a drink," the man insisted. "It's quiet now, but things are about to get busy. You not getting eaten in that tank confirm she's about ready."

Conrad didn't want a drink.

He wanted answers.

"Ready for what? Who are you? I already asked you these questions, and you're not answering them."

"I'm Dr. Hatcher. I'm an assistant director to this disaster. The director's out there cavorting around doing God knows what with his subjects. He's tried to kill me a handful of times. I guess he has bigger fish to fry now. Dr. Sutherland is insane. He hasn't been the same since the lampreys laid eggs in his brain. He's plugged into their collective consciousness. He wants what the lampreys want. Sutherland will see to it *she* gets off this rig and slithers into more populated areas. It would take only days, maybe a week, before half of the United States would be infected. They work fast because they're so hungry. They'll always be hankering for more flesh."

"Slow down, *please*," Conrad said, clutching his aching head. He'd been through hell, and there was no end of the ordeal in sight. "My family is here. They're in the military, sort of, and they've been forced to come here and fight these things. I bet they're looking for me. You could help them. But what happened to your side? You're bleeding. You need medical attention."

"I'm as good as dead," Dr. Hatcher sighed. "I was attacked by one of the smaller lampreys. I pulled it out in time, but those teeth, they spin and suck so fast. I lost a good chunk of meat. The bleeding hasn't stopped. It doesn't matter. I only wanted to live long enough to watch Mama leave this installation. It'll be a magnificent show. Her exodus will be so beautiful. If I'm going to go out, I'm going to see Mama bloom."

"Who is Mama?"

Dr. Hatcher pointed at the gigantic tank. "She's in there. You can't see her. The water hasn't been cleaned since the lampreys got out of control. Dr. Sutherland let the other ones out of their cages, and since then, we've all been on the menu."

"You mean there's a giant lamprey in there?"

"She probably weighs a few tons and Mama keeps on getting bigger."

"Why is she waiting in there? Why not bust out?"

"She can and she will, in good time. When she does, it's going to be a show to remember. You might as well drink up and relax while you still can. You're not getting off of this installation alive. Start letting that sink in. You won't survive. You're as good as dead."

Conrad pointed at the dry erase boards and the tables. He ignored the promises of death. "So you created these super lampreys? Why?"

"Why not?" Dr. Hatcher threw his head back and laughed. "And why not tell you what this is all about, huh? What else am I doing besides waiting to bleed out and for my buzz to kick in? You're not doing anything with the information. We're all doomed to die here. So fine, my team and I worked our asses off on this project. If it weren't for Dr. Sutherland letting them out of their cages and locking down the installation after they laid eggs in his brain, we would've succeeded."

Dr. Hatcher indulged in another drink.

"Why create super lampreys? Yes, the question of all questions. Think of it like this. It's funny how organic and all natural products have become the rage these days. It's trendy, saving the environment, isn't it? It's like wearing a fucking fanny pack."

Dr. Hatcher was starting to get drunk.

"Recycling, free range poultry, compost heaps, no GMOs, free trade, natural cleaners, they're all nice and dandy ideas, but one day, one distant day, hundreds and hundreds of years from now, using apple cider vinegar to clean your house and eating free range meat won't do a fucking thing to save the planet. We're delaying the inevitable. Hundreds, maybe thousands of years down the line, this planet is going to turn into a hot box of pollution. We won't be able to live on this planet, and the human race will die out. The earth will hit the reset button and we'll be extinct.

"My point is that the day will come when going organic isn't enough. Our research here is based on the need to clean up pollution by any means necessary. Forget morality, kindness, and popular opinion. We had to start somewhere, so we decided to start with our drinking water. Like our rivers, lakes, and streams, and then we'd expand to the oceans. We chose the lamprey because of their versatility. They normally feed on bacteria and other matter. Their suction mouths, their teeth, they're all perfect for sucking up pollution, so we enhanced them metabolically and physically. A lot of test tubes and growth hormones and steroids were injected into these lampreys. We designed them to have three stomachs, triple the teeth, the suction power of a thousand vacuums, and the ability to ingest and process paper, cardboard, and steel. They can shit it out just like everything else.

"We imagined them being freed in lakes and streams so they'd eat trash. If there's an oil spill, we can design them to suck up the oil from the water. Our team wasn't going to stop there. If this project was a success, we would've chosen birds to fly up so high in the sky they could fix our ozone layer. Smog in the bigger cities would be eliminated. Acid rain would be a thing of the past.

"TECHMODE, a private research entity, funded this project. They hired the topmost scientists to design a species of lamprey artificially that would exclusively eat pollution in our bodies of water. The problem, the lampreys preferred the taste of human flesh to garbage. They can't get enough meat. We tried to erase that instinct from their minds. That's what we've been working on here on this installation. It proved impossible.

"As we kept on with our research, Dr. Sutherland and other team members were attacked by the lampreys that were at the time the size of harmless snakes. They ate some of their victims alive, while others, like the good doctor, they plugged into their brains to control them. Dr. Chan, another assistant director, tried to call for outside help, but Dr. Sutherland had her killed and then had this place locked down. The lampreys have grown on their own, breeding and birthing in hours. They grow so fast it is impossible to stop them.

"TECHMODE is watching the facility through the security cameras. They're letting us die. They want to see the full extent of the lamprey and their abilities. They want to see Mama in that tank come to life. I've watched almost a dozen military teams come in here with their big guns and they die all the same. TECHMODE hired ENTECH to locate teams to wipe clean this installation so TECHMODE could start all over again. ENTECH's GI Joes can't do shit to stop the lampreys.

"TECHMODE waited too long to bring in the Calvary. They did that on purpose. TECHMODE does environmental research, but they also create biological weapons, you see? I guess this installation has turned into a testing ground for that new weapon. They've scrapped the anti-pollution idea altogether. Once big Mama leaves her tank, and they see the full extent of what she can accomplish, they're going to finally blow up this place. They figure ENTECH's hired guns will wipe out as many lampreys as possible and lower the risk of contamination. Then they'll take our research and sell it to the highest bidder. But if one of those things fall into the water and makes it to land, go ahead and kiss the human race goodbye. They're going to suck humanity of every ounce of flesh and blood until there's nothing left.

"They're so smart. They burrow into living vessels so they can travel from place to place when they're out of water. Human blood keeps them moist just like water. When that fails, they'll occupy anything, even dead corpses. They'll do absolutely anything to survive.

"But do I care? No not really. I'm dead soon, so fuck them. Fuck everyone. Once upon a time, I thought my work would do something positive for the world. I wanted to secure the environment for future generations to enjoy, but you know what? The human race would find another way to fuck it all up. The pollution-eating lampreys would be just an excuse to treat the environment like shit. So forget it. Let them all die. I'm done with humanity."

Conrad couldn't believe what he was hearing. "So you're just going to sit here and do nothing to save people's lives? You can help my father and his team kill the lampreys so they don't get off this rig and spread."

"I'm not doing a damn thing except drinking and watching big Mama's grand exit."

"*You won't even get to do that, Dr. Hatcher.*"

Dr. Sutherland had crept up behind Dr. Hatcher. The man's jaw was extended wide enough to clamp around Dr. Hatcher's entire head. Those spinning teeth, the mean crunching noises, the broken eggshell sounds, Dr. Hatcher's head was instantly liquefied. The mess was raucously sucked up into Sutherland's throat. Dr. Hatcher's body did a nervous jig as spurts of blood sprayed from his serrated neck stump.

Dr. Sutherland stepped back, lifted up his shirt, and exposed that hideous maw jagged with teeth. The doctor's midsection was tight with new muscles as the mouth started to suction air. Dr. Hatcher's body bent in half from the maw's sucking force. The doctor's hip and pelvic bones crunched and shattered. Bones burst beneath his skin. Arms and legs were wrenched off with such uncouth power. Dr. Hatcher's remains were in ten pieces when they were dragged up into that vicious belly-mouth and devoured.

Conrad fell off his chair and was now crawling backwards. He cried out when his back hit the glass of the aquarium. He sensed vibrations through the glass. He couldn't see Mama, but Conrad knew she was stirring in those mysterious depths.

"Dr. Hatcher is doing more good in my stomach than he ever did on the field," Dr. Sutherland rasped. "When I tried to convince him to side with Mama, Dr. Hatcher refused, so I said have it your way. One day, we'll feed on you. He didn't believe letting them inside his body was for the best, so all the bad for him. I'm sure it doesn't feel good to be eaten alive, *but it sure feels fine doing the eating!*"

Conrad gawked at the doctor's changing face. His mouth and belly had reverted back to normal, but his eyes were still hidden deep in the chasms of his sockets. Teeth circled his sockets. They clicked together as if ready to devour anything at a moment's notice.

"When the world succumbs to the lampreys, it'll be people like me they treat like a god. I gave them a life, and I'll give them safe passage off this rig. I will always be there to give them the meat they crave.

"*Ooooooh*, I can feel them moving in my brain. They give me such pleasure. I've never felt so good in my life. Sex, drugs, booze, it's nothing compared to what it feels like to have them living inside me. They reward the subservient. I am their willing vessel. No harm must come to Mama. Without her, they're nothing. Without her, I'm nothing. I will never be nothing again. I'M KING OF THE LAMPREYS!"

Conrad choked back the urge to vomit. Dr. Sutherland's eyes kept popping up, looking around, and then sinking back into his skull. The teeth continued retracting and retracting, seemingly matching the fervor of his words. The doctor was insane. He was also infested. The skin along his neck, cheeks, even his scalp, was bubbling and boiling with lampreys shifting beneath the flesh.

"So will you join us? Let us infest you."

Popping up from the skin, dozens of lampreys stuck out of the doctor's arms, back, and neck. Dr. Sutherland was a walking medusa.

Conrad didn't have to say a word. He retreated to the opposite end of the room. After passing lab tables and empty aquariums of all sizes, Conrad located an open door. Before he stormed out of the room, he could hear Mama splash in her aquarium.

Whatever was going to happen, it was going down soon.

Conrad had to find his family, tell them everything he knew about the lampreys, and somehow get the hell off of this installation.

He prayed Dr. Sutherland didn't follow after him.

Chapter Twenty-Four

Henry's team couldn't fall back. The doors to the new room closed themselves. There was no escape. Henry couldn't show fear. The only thing he could do was raise his Gatling gun and take down as many of them as he could. Everybody else on the team had the same idea. Dirty Poncho struck a series of green flares he'd taken from the steel box. He hoped the bright light would ward off the impossible creatures.

The burning sticks did nothing.

Working together, the Gatling gun barrels spun, spewing bullets, death, and noise. They straight away featured shattered holding tanks big enough to hold dozens of people. The team crunched over glass as they dared to step deeper into the mysterious research room. They thought they had driven back the first group of fiendish monsters, but they were wrong.

They were suddenly surrounded. Winds blasted throughout the room. It felt like a tornado was attacking the area. Henry clutched onto his gun tighter so the weapon wouldn't be wrenched from his clutches.

Black-skinned lampreys crawled on the floor. They ranged in sizes from anacondas to giant sewer pipes. Countless numbers slithered forth, advancing like stealthy eels.

Henry instructed at the top of his lungs. "Scoop, you keep the ones on the floor busy!"

Holes were punched into the ceiling. Tiles rained down and lamprey heads the size of human beings, if not bigger, would poke their sucker faces down and hiss. Hot rubber glue-like saliva rained down in pelting wads. The teeth in their circular mouths spun at shredding speeds. Keyes' hair shot up into the air one second, and the next, her neck was stretched until the head completely broke off. Spinning up to the ceiling, the head landed in the creature's maw and it was instantly liquefied.

Fryer cried out, "No! Goddamn all of you!"

Fryer put down his Gatling gun.

"No, Fryer, keep firing your guns! You can't do anything for Keyes now."

Scoop picked up Keyes' dropped Gatling gun and was firing both at the same time. She could barely hold herself up. The fear and determination on Scoop's face kept those barrels spitting fire.

Fryer grabbed Keyes' headless body by the waist. "*Noooooooooo!* You're not taking her, you slimy fucking bastards!"

Fryer and Keyes were both sucked up into the ceiling. Henry reeled seeing both bodies enter an insane paper shredder. Fryer's legs were still kicking until his feet were the only thing remaining of him. Then the rest of him was sucked up and consumed.

Scoop laughed, "They were fucking useless anyway!"

A hole in the ceiling was punched above Duke's head.

"Son! Up top!"

Duke saw the hideous lamprey's sticky maw widen to take him in.

"Fuck you!" Duke unfastened a grenade from his belt, undid the pin, and hurled it upwards. The lamprey's powerful suction had no problem sucking up the grenade.

Three seconds later, a muffled POP sounded. A large section of the ceiling caved in, and the lamprey crashed down onto the floor bleeding from its middle and mouth. From the opening, jellied pieces of the human anatomy kicked up a wretched stink.

"Scoop," Henry shouted, "empty some rounds into the ceiling. Keep them busy for a moment. Duke, you, me, and Poncho keep blasting what's ahead of us."

They made short work of the smaller lampreys on the floor. When bullets didn't work, they stomped them with their boots. Henry thought the enemies were weakening. That was until a new horde charged forth in a collective front. Hundreds of them were angling after the team.

They weren't lampreys this time.

They were human beings, and they were altered.

The subjects were naked. The scientists hadn't given them the respect of decency. Henry unleashed a battle cry as one of the men ran right up to him with a hideous lamprey sucker over his mouth about to bear down on his body. Henry jammed the Gatling gun barrels into the mouth and injected the monster with enough hot lead to send its throat out its ass.

Dirty Poncho hurled a grenade when the skin over a woman's belly flapped up like a window shade. Six snakes of intestines shot forth at him, each end of pink viscera chomping at the bit with lamprey suckers and dagger teeth. The grenade turned the intestines into pureed pink.

Scoop shot the heads off ten enemies in a row, only for the bodies to lower their necks and show off the rings of teeth along their clavicle bones. Henry punched bullets through those monsters, leaving battered bodies strewn on the floor.

"Please, kill me!"

"I only want to die!"

"For God's sake, show us mercy!"

"I'm hideous."

"I never wanted to kill anybody."

"They've turned us into murdering cannibals."

"I can't stop eating flesh!"

"Meat, meat, meat, MEAT! *Ahahahahahahahahaha!*"

Henry blinked and blinked. Maybe if he kept blinking, he could erase the insanity of the images and what he was hearing from the lips of the suffering.

This was really happening, Henry kept telling himself, and there was only one thing he could do. Henry fulfilled his obligation as a sane and rational person, raised his gun, and unleashed a flood of rip-roaring Gatling gun bullet-fire.

A long line of people almost fifty long were connected at the hip like Siamese twins by a lamprey so long and stretched thin. The black snake pulsed with thick muscles and power. Every victim wore heightened modes of terror on their faces. Their hands and feet were shackled by chains. After the first string of bullets punched their bodies, the lamprey slipped free of each body. The god-awful sounds of slithering meat, breaking bones, and the wails of agony from the victims was almost too much to take, but Henry would be damned if he would end up as meat to be shit out some creature's asshole or a prisoner of some sick scientific anatomical study.

The long and thin lamprey wound itself up like a cobra snake. Its maw elongated to the size of a doorway. Sucker face stretched to its limits, those horrible teeth spinning with mechanical speed. The resulting suction grabbed each of the victims. The group of fifty went airborne, slashing at empty air to avoid being diced to death. It happened in seconds. The great lamprey sucked fifty of them into its dangerous mouth and acted like a meat grinder on acid. Out its hidden anus, bones fired and pinged against the wall. By the end of it, there was a tall hill of gnarled broken skeletal pieces.

"Everybody, GRE-NADE!"

Henry, Duke, Scoop, and Dirty Poncho hurled grenades at the large lamprey.

Quadruple booms later, sections of the floor opened up, giving away to flaming steel. The lamprey had fallen through the hole. Strings of black flesh dangled from the edges of the hole. Dead or not, the beast was out of their way.

There were other monsters in the room, but their gunfire had crippled them. They were other subjects from a long line of diabolical tests.

"This is Hitler shit," Dirty Poncho said, as he emptied rounds into a woman's belly whose "baby" was a bowling ball sized group of string-thin lampreys. "How could anybody get away with this? This is sick."

"Private research," Scoop answered. "It's funded by non-government entities. They don't have to be regulated. They can avoid following the rules. It's not until something catastrophic occurs that things like this gets noticed, and by then, it's much too late. The victims are already piled high."

Scoop was startled when two hands grabbed her Gatling gun barrels. The lamprey man shoved the barrels into his mouth and nodded his head in approval.

Scoop pulled the trigger.

She winced seeing the man's eyes trained on her until they burst out of his head.

Dirty Poncho stomped a lamprey with two human heads on both ends of its body.

"I can only imagine what they had in mind when committing to this research," Duke said. "You give up your soul doing this to innocent people."

"Money," Scoop said. "I did enough investigative reporting in my early days. It's always the same. Sex or money, but most often, money wins over every other human impulse. Amati was a good man, and he too had his price, didn't he?"

"We're not Amati," Henry said. "Clean sweep the area, and then we keep moving. Conrad's out there all alone. God knows what he's seen by now."

The team went about finishing off the disheartening remains of the test subjects. Scoop and Dirty Poncho had the misfortune of coming across the young woman with lamprey mouths over both her breasts and her vagina. The expression of "why me?" stayed on her face until enough bullets entered her body to sever all brain function.

When the room was nothing but blood and dead bodies, Henry brought his team together again. The only entry into the room was also the room's only exit. Dirty Poncho worked on disengaging the room's key panel.

"No go, sir," Dirty Poncho said. "Someone's locked us in."

"THAT'S RIGHT YOU'RE LOCKED IN! EVERYTHING YOU DO WORKS TO MY ADVANTAGE. YOU THINK I'M GOING TO LET YOU STOP HER? SHE'S LEAVING SOON. MAMA NEEDS A FEW HUNDRED MORE POUNDS OF MEAT FOR THE ROAD. IT'LL TAKE A LOT OF ENERGY TO SWIM TO TEXAS. IT WORKED OUT GREAT THAT THEY KEEP BRINGING IN MORE PEOPLE LIKE YOU TO FEED MY CREATION."

Henry saw the hole in the floor from when the grenades went off earlier. "Quick, in there!"

Before any of the team could react, the ceiling broke into dozens of pieces. The walls on every side of them crumbled, smashed in from the other side. Black slippery bodies, widening death maws, teeth angling to spin and suck; lampreys that could double as sewer pipes were incoming. Suction force attacked them from every angle.

Steel cages were dragged from across the room and sucked up into the ceiling. Dangerous teeth bent, warped, and ingested steel. Human cages were crushed by powerful gusts of air and reduced to splinters by the time the teeth made short work of the remains. Lab desks, life support machines, refrigerators full of mysterious chemicals imploded and exploded. The chamber of horrors was emptied of every object. Henry's team was the only thing that remained. Henry forced Duke to jump down into the biggest hole in the floor first.

"Go!"

The suction attached itself to Henry. He felt the tug against his scalp, then the pull on his arms and legs. He fired the Gatling gun. The bullets were redirected midstream and sucked up into the monster's maw.

Henry couldn't believe it.

The suction was strong enough to stop bullets.

"MOVE OUT NOW!"

Scoop jumped down into the hole next.

A jagged line of flesh from Henry's scalp down to his jaw was ripped. He watched in awe as the bolt of flesh spun and soared into a lamprey's gaping mouth.

Dirty Poncho escaped next.

Henry's Gatling gun was pried from his hands. The lamprey above him chomped the steel and sucked it down like a garbage disposal from hell.

Suctions of air, alarming undercurrents of power, Henry was about to jump down next when a lamprey mouth filled in the hole. Henry prayed his team made it down alive. Holes were punctured into the walls and floor in increasing fervor. Henry's face was bleeding. The exposed meat along Henry's scalp blazed with pain. Henry gritted his teeth. He reached down to his belt, removed two Bowie combat knives, and clutched them to kill.

Chapter Twenty-Five

Conrad refused to stop moving. He had no destination in mind except for escape. The longer he fled from Dr. Sutherland, the more it troubled him. Where was he supposed to go? He had no map to this giant place. Dr. Sutherland could be waiting around any corner, and worse, the lampreys could eat his ass up any second. Conrad charged up a flight of emergency stairs, then rushed back down when the exit leading to the other floors were locked. He double backed, stalked new hallways where the doors were each locked, and ended up going across a long bridge that connected to another building. What he found here were living quarters. Doors were broken off their hinges. Blood painted every surface. Gaping holes damaged the floors and ceilings. He had to watch his step or else turn his ankle or fall completely through to whatever was below.

He froze when he heard footsteps rattle the floor. Not really footsteps, Conrad thought, more like somebody shambling along: *one step, two step, dr-aaaaaag.*

A shadow limped out of one of the rooms down the hall. First, Conrad heard something slither, then the wet smacking sound of meat being squished together. He couldn't move. Conrad recognized who this person was and he was mortified.

Bavardi.

But not Bavardi.

Half of his face was missing to be replaced by balled up lamprey bodies. Most of his skull was open to the air. Lampreys stuck out of his gray matter like amphibious circuitry. Bavardi's broken bones were fastened together by a rough collection of lamprey bodies. In Bavardi's arms, he cradled random appendages and leftovers from several dead, severely mangled bodies.

Conrad ducked into the shadows at the last moment before Bavarti could spot him. He held his breath and did his best to maintain calm. That was impossible when he heard other sounds of movement throughout the living quarters. Men and women in lab coats, about six of them, were going in and out of rooms carrying severed limbs and wet entrails. These people were exactly like Bavardi. Most of their bodies had been severely devoured or mutilated. Lamprey bodies had infested their corpses to create walking, working slaves. That work collectively involved stacking up leftovers from a previous slaughter. Whatever didn't get sucked up or ingested by the lampreys from before wouldn't go to waste.

Bavardi was the at the very edge of the hallway. He was closing in on Conrad's location. Bavardi's one eye noticed Conrad. The corpse's face froze, except for the writhing of lamprey bodies stuffed in his eye socket and brains. Conrad had no idea what the man would have to say to him in his current state.

"Your father is a good man," Bavardi said, his voice without affectation. The man was a zombie. "He gave me a chance when everybody thought I was crazy. When I don't take my medications, all I see is violence. They tortured me to the very end of my sanity. Goddamn terrorists. Goddamn caves. Nobody comes out of being tortured the same. I did my best to control the beast, and I'm so sorry for what I did to you back at that hotel. None of that matters, because the lampreys are taking me over!"

The lampreys sticking out of Bavardi's brains tensed up and dug themselves deeper into his exposed gray matter. Bavardi's body went into spasms. Whatever human part of Bavardi came up to the surface, it was quickly buried under intense agony.

"I am their vessel," automaton Bavardi said. "I am theirs to use."

The ceiling over the great pile of body parts the human slaves had stacked up suddenly shifted. A lamprey the size of an anaconda hovered over the pile and sucked up every scrap in its spinning maw. More punches into the ceiling, five more lampreys poked their enormous sucker faces down into the hallway. The piercing whistle of air suctioned at insane speeds was a wicked screech to Conrad's ears.

Bavardi removed a long cylindrical grenade from his belt.

He came to himself again.

"No, you can't control me! Al Qaeda couldn't break me, and neither can you, lampreys! My mind is stronger than you are. You can take my body, but you can't take my mind. Run, Conrad! I'll buy you time. Go! Turn your head. The flash grenade will blind you. Now move your ass, solider!"

Bavardi's hand pushed Conrad down the other side of the hall. Conrad picked up his feet. He heard a great BOOM and a flash of bluish light filled the area.

The lampreys screeched against the flash grenade's burst of light. Conrad cleared four halls. Gunfire echoed through the muffling barriers of walls. It could be his father and the rest of his team. They could be alive. That meant there was still hope of surviving.

From one end of the hall, Conrad heard the dead lamprey-infested zombies and the lampreys themselves stalk after him. Up ahead, hundreds of lampreys the size of garden snakes slithered between the walls and the ceiling searching for food.

Conrad shot up the nearest staircase, ascended a level, and ran to the nearest door. This door was unlocked. He threw it shut, barricaded it with a long table, and put his back to it. Conrad waited and listened to see if anything would bang on the other side of the door to get him.

Several minutes passed, and all he heard was machinegun fire. When that stopped, he swore he heard a man howl in rage.

Conrad swore that man was his father.

Fists beat against the door before he could think too long on his father.

Lampreys were trying to squeeze through the crack of the door.

"I couldn't hold them back," Bavardi shouted outside the door. "I'll do what I can, but you have to get out of this room, Conrad, and fast!"

Holes burst in the door. Lamprey sucker faces hissed and spun their teeth as they slithered through the broken wood to attack. Conrad saw the bloody, mutilated faces of the lamprey infested walking corpses. Bavardi was holding them back, pushing them back, head butting them, and then collapsing when the lampreys re-claimed control of his body. But Bavardi wouldn't give up. He surged right back up to his feet to force back the small pack of aggressors.

Conrad searched the room for any options of escape. There was a steel door open a crack. It had a key panel code. He wouldn't need a password, and thank God, Conrad thought, because that was his only option to avoid oncoming death.

Retreating out of the room, he opened the steel door, and then quickly threw the steel door shut. He locked it and waited. Conrad shivered in the room. It was freezing cold. He scanned the wall for a light switch. When he turned on the overhead light, Conrad gasped in horror.

Chapter Twenty-Six

Scoop was crawling on her hands and knees in a duct system. She kept moving as fast as she could. Dirty Poncho was right behind her. She yelled to ask him if Henry and Duke were behind them. Dirty Poncho said no. He had no idea what happened to them. They were on their own. The mission was going to shit.

Scoop thought, *Fuck you Amati; fuck you very much. Enjoying that money ENTECH paid you? I bet it spends well in hell! The only way out of this situation was to be devoured by a fucking fish.*

The duct was growing hotter. There was no air actively flowing through it. She had lost her Gatling gun escaping that room. Scoop had a knife, maybe a grenade, and that was about it. That would do nothing to help them get out of here alive. Maybe they could find a flotation device, find a way off this rig, and hope the ocean carried them to land.

Impossible, she kept thinking. Death would be the final outcome. They were stuck here against a horde of hungry lampreys.

How could they survive?

Scoop's elbows and knees ached from being rubbed raw. How far did the duct system go before showing a way out? The installation was huge. She couldn't imagine what part of the rig they were crawling to or from.

Why would ENTECH do this to them? Henry and his team were loyal to the cause of humanitarian efforts. Why throw them into this trap without being fully prepared?

Henry had said it earlier, she remembered. ENTECH was compromised. Scoop doubted she'd live long enough to learn the depth of the betrayal and the reasons for mutated lampreys to exist.

If she was going to die, she was going to take out as many of those lampreys as possible.

A square of light appeared up ahead, giving a break in the darkness.

Scoop moved faster.

"Up ahead, Poncho. We're almost out of here."

Dirty Poncho unleashed a yelp of pain in response. The sound of something wet and slithering like a giant slug sliding down a piece of sheet metal was stalking them. A suction of air forced Scoop to brace her feet and arms against the walls of the ducts. Dirty Poncho held on for his life as well. Scoop turned around and could see Poncho's horrified face. His mouth was wide in horror as his scalp and face were peeled backwards and sucked into the hideous lamprey's maw. Her comrade's head was uprooted from the neck in a symphony of bones cracking and muscles tearing. Headless, the rest of Dirty Poncho was dragged into the merciless void of spinning teeth and insatiable hunger.

Dirty Poncho was gone.

The body was reduced to liquid in seconds.

Then the suction was on Scoop in full force. Scoop lunged forward, grabbed hold of the opened air vent and pulled herself up with all of her might. Straining her body, almost to the point her muscles gave out, Scoop did a forward flip, and dropped straight down into an unknown room.

The lamprey beast was still incoming. She was meat to be eaten. Scoop did the only thing she could do. Scoop unstrapped the last grenade on her belt. She pulled the pin, counted to two, and tossed up the grenade into the open vent.

BA-BOOM!

Scoop stayed back from the vent. She coughed against the smoke filling up the room. She wasn't sure if her timing was right or if the creature had steered clear of the grenade.

Her question was soon answered. A lamprey the size of a smart car crashed into the room. Its sucker face was a sizzling stump of bleeding meat. The smell reminded her of bacon crossed with salmon.

Scoop was choking against the smoke and the cooked lamprey stench.

There was only one door out of the room.
Scoop didn't have to think.
She exited the room with haste.

Chapter Twenty-Seven

Henry had no idea if the blood crossing his lips was *theirs* or his own. The room was jam-packed with enemies. Everything was in constant motion, including him. Henry vaulted forward, slashing both his Bowie knives in wide-spanning arcs. One blade scraped against teeth. The other blade slashed one of the anaconda-sized lampreys across the belly up to its sucker mouth. Everything inside of it spilled forth in a wave of cold disgusting mess. Henry was thrown up against a wall. Two dozen, thirty, maybe fifty of the lampreys occupied the room, and each of them was trying to suction him into their hungry maws. Henry was reduced to a ragdoll caught in the airstream of too many enemies.

The assault was dizzying and Henry had no control over his body. He did his best to keep slashing his combat knives to ward them back. The sleeve of his shirt was torn. A large X of skin was sucked from his back.

Henry roared with pain.

Those sensations drove him to extremes. He pivoted his body just right to avoid their suction for two seconds. Henry dropped to the floor and rolled to the nearest lamprey.

"You think you can kill me? I'd like to see you fucking try!"

Henry crept up behind the lamprey that was as tall as his body and almost as thick. He jammed both Bowie knives below its sucker face. Henry had control of it. Using it like a puppet, he pivoted its maw towards the other lampreys.

The lamprey's teeth were spinning and suctioning air even faster in a panic. The creature didn't know how to ward off the attack, so it kept sucking, and sucking, and sucking with insane power. Sonic booms and loud percussions filled the room. Henry pointed the sucker face at every creature.

The lampreys attacking him were knocked backwards, shoved into each other, thrown into the ceiling, and collided into each other. Air streams worked against the lampreys, tearing squares of meat from their bodies. Blood and black amphibious flesh flew across the room, suctioning to random mouths who all sucked in confusion.

Henry's trick had worked so well, the lampreys began to retreat. When every last one of them were gone, Henry dragged the Bowie knives down the lamprey's body until he'd sliced it up enough it stopped thrashing and fighting.

When the dead lamprey struck the floor, Henry couldn't believe he had survived. The rest of his team's whereabouts was unknown. How was he going to bring them together again?

Where to go next was another burning question.

"QUITE AN IMPRESSIVE SHOW. YOUR TEAM WON'T FARE AS WELL AS YOU DID. YOU CAN KILL AS MANY AS YOU LIKE, BUT YOU WON'T STOP MAMA. ONCE SHE'S HAD HER FINAL MEAL, WE'LL BE LEAVING THIS INSTALLATION. BY THEN, YOU'LL BE NOTHING MORE THAN FUEL FOR HER TRAVELS. YOUR SUCCULENT MEAT WILL SERVE HER WELL ON HER JOURNEY TO AMERICAN SOIL.

"NOBODY CAN STOP HER. SHE'LL GIVE BIRTH TO MORE CREATURES ON LAND, AND THEY'LL FEED ON THE MASSES. SO GO AHEAD AND LOOK FOR THE REST OF YOUR FRIENDS. YOU'RE NOTHING AGAINST US."

The steel doors out of the room opened.

"I GIVE YOU FREE REIN. THE EASIER YOU FIND US, THE EASIER IT'LL BE FOR US TO FIND YOU AND EAT YOU."

Henry was dripping blood from head to toe. This time, he knew whose blood was pasted to his body. He stalked out of the room, clutching both knives, and searched in every direction to make sure none of the lampreys would ambush him.

He had many tasks to complete. The first, locate the rest of his team, and then he'd search for Conrad, and figure out a way to get off of this installation alive.

Henry also had another mission.

He had to find the man talking to them over the intercom system.

Chapter Twenty-Eight

Through the towel draped over his face, Bavardi could sense the evil people in the room who poured buckets of water over his head. Water was choking him through his nostrils and going down his throat. They were water boarding him. Hours and hours of torture, Bavardi was on the verge of drowning and then saved just in the nick of time, only to be put through the same hell again and again. How many long nights had he spent in the dark without food and water? He hadn't slept in days, maybe weeks. How could he sleep? When he was strapped into the chair, water was dripped on his head. Each drop hit him every thirty seconds. The drops of water made it impossible to sleep.

The terrorist bastards in the cave were merciless. They forced Bavardi to watch as they eviscerated and cut American soldiers into pieces. Bavardi was forced to sit in this very room with their putrid, expiring bodies, and still, they hadn't broke him. The terrorists didn't want secrets from him. They wanted to break an American solider. They wished for Bavardi to condemn his own country. The bastards' goal was for him to shove a gun into his mouth and blow out his brains. He wouldn't. The longer they couldn't break him, the more they wanted to break Bavardi. It was a sick, never-ending twisted game.

Weeks into his ordeal, nobody was coming to save him. That's when one night he broke free of his binds. The only weapon he had were his fists and his brains. He strangled men. Bavardi had nearly ripped off another man's mandible in a rage. When he was armed with an AK-47, he mowed down dozens of the bastards.

The terrorists wouldn't break him.

They failed.

But the lampreys...

I am their vessel.
I serve to feed Mama.

Bavardi was seized by another wave of pain as the lampreys bored into his brain. He was fighting the other people invaded by the lampreys. They had smashed through the door to get to Conrad. Now he was alone in the hallway. He was in limbo between giving in to the lampreys and fighting back.

He sensed others like him throughout the installation invading rooms, picking up whatever human pieces had been missed from previous slaughters, and stacking them up in hallways for the lampreys to devour.

I am a vessel.
I serve to feed Mama.

After being captured by the terrorists, Bavardi had changed. His family didn't recognize him. His wife divorced him. He never saw his daughter, Melinda, ever again. He withdrew from his family and friends. He knew the evils of the world, and he was consumed by them.

However, Henry saved him. Henry knew his pain, because he too had been tortured in Vietnam. He carried the scars and the memories and somehow turned his life into a mission of positivity and peace. Without Henry, Bavardi would've died a long time ago.

He had to do something to save Henry and his team, but *oh my God, the agony!* The squishing of his brains, the lampreys denied him cognitive thought and bodily control.

Mama is hungry.
She must feed.
I am her vessel.

Bavardi was a drone once again. He kicked in doors, and searched rooms and labs for bits and pieces of the human body that could be salvaged and consumed.

Chapter Twenty-Nine

Duke had crawled in the opposite direction as Scoop and Dirty Poncho. Fighting his way in the duct system, it wasn't long before a lamprey was stalking him. He clutched his Gatling gun and pounded the creature's face full of hot lead. Teeth, blood, and black amphibious tissue was chewed up until the face was only a nasty stump. More of them would be on their way, so Duke doubled his efforts to escape. His speed was significantly slowed from carrying the machine gun.

Did his father make it out of that laboratory? Duke knew his father could take care of himself in a sticky situation. Conrad, on the other hand, was a book reading wimp who wanted to sit on the sidelines and analyze everything through discussions instead of real actions. He loved making fun of his brother, because he loved his brother. Duke hadn't told him that, except for when his parents made him do it as a kid. Brothers didn't really say that to each other, but after going through this, Duke needed to tell Conrad he cared.

If Conrad was alive to hear it.

Duke kept banging his head and his elbows against the walls. He heard wild peals of pain from the other end of the duct system. Dirty Poncho was being attacked. Probably dead, by the agonizing octaves the man unleashed.

He kept moving.

Two ideas kept flashing in his mind.

Find Conrad.

Kill the lampreys.

Suddenly the duct system couldn't handle his weight. His angle was titled straight down, and the flat surface turned into a downward slide. Duke spun forward. He clutched onto his gun, refusing to let go of his only weapon besides a Bowie knife.

Falling through empty air, he was being dropped from high up. Duke braced himself for a rough landing. He was right to do so. After slamming into a deck made of solid wood, Duke thought he broke some ribs, and maybe his left arm. Attacked by wild conflagrations of pain, Duke absorbed it and did his best to live it down so he could survey his surroundings and ensure his safety.

Duke heard the running of a waterfall. He smelled wet wood, dead bodies, and stranger yet, a chemical mix that was a cross between bleach and citronella. The whiff crossed his nose as wrong and unnatural.

The pain leveled out. He wasn't as injured as he first thought. Duke hadn't broken his arm, but his ribs were very sore. He clutched onto his Gatling gun and searched high and low for anything. He stood on a wooden deck that overlooked a giant pool of water. Judging by how high the deck was, the pool was at least eight to twelve feet deep and twice as big as an Olympic pool. The water was neon green and glowing. Large machines filtered out the water connected to black barrels marked with biohazard symbols. The pool had a steel covering that was retracted over the top. Somebody had left the pool open.

"Thank God, you're here," somebody said nearby. "It might be too late for me, but you can still save the rest of the world. They won't know what hit them if a single one of the lampreys gets off of this rig. Humanity wouldn't stand a chance."

Duke found the speaker. He demanded the woman in her mid-fifties identify herself.

"I'm   Dr.   Locke."
"What's your hand in this project?"

"I oversaw the injection of chemicals into our specimens. I made sure our lampreys received enough doses of Terazin-L to grow new stomachs, teeth, and a voracious hunger to consume pollution. I've been hiding and hoping somebody arrived here to save us. Everybody before you didn't make it five minutes before being slaughtered."

"How did everybody get killed in the first place?" Duke asked.

"We had the lampreys under lock and key," Dr. Locke insisted. She pointed in the other direction. Other glass tanks of various sizes had their tops unlocked and were left wide open. "But they could always get out. Dr. Sutherland just made it so they escaped all at once...*so we could all die at once.* Some of us survived in hiding. I knew my time would come to be devoured. I wish I had known you were here sooner. I wouldn't have made a poor decision."

The woman was very pale. Her eyes were leaking green tears. She was hugging herself and constantly trembling as if in a fever.

"What did you do? Tell me. Maybe I can help you."

Dr. Locke bent over the edge of the wooden deck and pointed down into the neon water. "This chemical, Terazin-L, advances digestive systems. Right now, I feel new intestines growing in my belly." She pulled up her top to reveal a bulging stomach. "It hurts so bad. Everything's been stretched and compacted. Oh, my God, look at my hands!"

A slit cut itself down the middle of her palm. Between the vaginal slits, they slowly turned into circular maws armed with pointy teeth.

"Run! I can't stop it. I shouldn't have drunk the chemical! I thought it would help me fight them. *I was so stupid; I was so scared!*"

Dr. Locke's voice metamorphosed into a monstrous growling, "*I'm so hun-gry!*" Her eyes were forced out of her head and dangled from meaty strings. Her nose sank into her face and vanished. The woman's jaw and mandible crunched and cracked as it transformed. Skin twisted and tore, allowing the woman's mouth to turn sideways. Down the middle of her features was a giant drooling sucker mouth. That mouth ate the woman's own hanging eyeballs and champed at the empty air hankering for something more substantial.

Duke took action. He scissor kicked the woman into the green water. The woman sank into the green and disappeared. That's when her demented moans of hunger upgraded into screams. The chemical pool kept changing her body. Every inch of her split and tore to form new sucker maws. Those maws bit and sucked, tearing and shredding the woman into so many pieces until what was left of her sank to the bottom of the pool.

He wasn't sticking around to see anything else. Duke rushed down the stairwell. The landing below was littered with hundreds of glass tanks. The ones that weren't opened from the top had been shattered completely. Green stains marked the floor. Terazin-L, he imagined. Between the tanks were rubber hoses that Duke assumed fed the toxic water into each glass tank.

Duke kept picturing the woman's body covered in a dozen mouths, and each of them viciously trying to cannibalize the other.

This is what happens when crazy people have money.

Deeper in the room was a passage with thick Plexiglas walls. It faced the pool of green water. He imagined scientists watching the lampreys morph and mutate into eating machines. Computers and equipment that belonged in a mad scientist's laboratory took up much of the room.

Nothing useful here, he thought.

Duke located a side door that was open. It led back into the same narrow hallways they'd encountered earlier throughout the installation.

Right after he crossed the threshold, the door behind him slammed closed.

The intercom rattled Duke. "MAMA'S STILL HUNGRY. SHE WANTS EACH AND EVERY ONE OF YOU INSIDE HER!"

Duke braced himself, clutching the Gatling gun. He heard the dragging of feet. A collection of people was coming after him. Duke was up against a wall. The only direction to go was forward, and the group in the hallway took up any other way of escape. There were more scientists, each severely mutilated. Duke wasn't sure how they could function or surpass death to live.

The collection of lampreys burrowing and holding them together answered that disturbing question.

Jesus, the lampreys can do almost anything.

Bigger lampreys were shifting and traveling in the walls and ceiling. Duke could hear them over the din of the incoming horde.

Duke pulled back the trigger and realized he was out of bullets.

"Fuck. *Fuck!*"

He threw down the gun and clutched his Bowie knife. Duke knew he wasn't going to fare well in a hand-to-hand combat situation. The best way to fight them was to stay the hell away from them.

With not much time to think, Duke tried to find a route to race past them. It was impossible. Fifteen of them spread out, forming a sort of a wall. Duke would have no choice but to fight them.

He was seconds from slashing his knife across the closest throat when a familiar person came out of the collection and said, *"I'll hold them back for as long as I can. I know where your father is!"*

Chapter Thirty

Conrad shivered in the room that turned out to be a giant freezer. He couldn't open the door from this side. He was trapped. The zombie/lamprey monsters stopped banging against the outside of the door. They, for whatever reason, moved on to something else. Conrad didn't have a chance to enjoy the safe moment, because the freezer was full of dead bodies. They were dressed up in lab coats, each of them clustered together hugging onto one another as if their collective body heat could save them from the cold. He didn't have to think long on the fourteen corpses and why they were in here. Conrad imagined the lampreys attacking, and the scientists choosing the closest safe place, and this cold box was it.

A dark thought crept into his mind.

You're going to die in here too.

Conrad couldn't get over the way the skin of the dead shined with frost. It saddened him to see such desperation in their moment of death.

The rest of the room was full of tall steel shelves mostly stocked with food supplies. There was little room to avoid the dead bodies. That's all Conrad could look at was death.

But they had to know this was dangerous. They created these things. Why weren't they more careful?

Dr. Hatcher said the lampreys were designed to eat pollution. It was hard to believe creatures like lampreys could be trusted not to do more than just eat pollution.

He remembered Dr. Sutherland and Bavardi. They were both occupied by the lampreys, each controlled and possessed. These scientists had no choice in the matter, because the lampreys were smarter than anyone ever anticipated.

Conrad shivered in the cold. He could dissect why this had happened, and how people could let research like this spiral out of control, but none of it mattered. He would die in this frigid tomb. End of story.

Another voice popped into his head.

Duke's.

You're being a big pussy.

"I am not a big pussy! Just because I'm not like you and Dad doesn't mean what I do with my life is shit. It's cold, I'm alone, I'm single, I'm unemployed, and my fiancé fucked the whole world without me knowing it!"

Conrad pushed down a food shelf in a fit of rage. If he could do life again, he thought, as every person thought faced with death, he would live life differently. He was only thirty-two years old. He had more life to live. He'd find a better woman to marry. He could write that novel he was trying to pen for five years now— and this place had given him plenty of emotions to draw from— and teach the meanest literature class any college had ever experienced. He would blow the students off of their desks!

If only he could escape.

He stomped on the shelf, bursting open packages of frozen vegetables. When he was done with his angry fit, he was out of breath and realized how pointless it was to act out. Getting in touch with his emotions did nothing but affirm death was looming.

Wait, what is that?

Conrad traced it with his eyes. It was the outline of a door. That outline was crusted with ice. It couldn't be a doorway, he thought. He touched the outline with his finger. It wasn't his imagination. Conrad located a small mechanism that resembled a car door's handle and opened the door. He walked through the door and was relieved to feel room temperature air again. Conrad shut the door. What he'd found was a secret passage. The short hallway led to a single doorway. That doorway was cracked open. He couldn't resist. He walked inside the room and discovered more horror.

Chapter Thirty-One

Dr. Sutherland was standing in one of four security rooms located throughout the installation. He studied the wall of televisions, monitoring the intruders' progress. Every lamprey inside him was squirming beneath his skin anticipating Mama's travels. He pinpointed the whereabouts of Henry, Scoop, Conrad, and Duke. The lampreys were swiftly stalking them. Soon, nobody would be left alive to stop them. He had to act fast. Soon, ENTECH, or TECHMODE, or whoever was watching the show from another shore, would send in rockets to turn this place into a big burning inferno.

He wasn't sure what TECHMODE or ENTECH were up to now. Dr. Sutherland did know this. The lampreys wouldn't be used for environmental purposes anymore. They would be used as a weapon. Who needed atom bombs and nuclear technology when you could infest an entire nation in a matter of weeks?

Dr. Sutherland exited the security checkpoint and returned to the lab where Mama waited in her tank. He could barely see her gargantuan profile in the dark waters. Mama pressed her sucker face against the glass wall. Her mouth was almost three stories tall. People could be impaled from anus to their heads on those teeth. And the suction power, he hadn't had the opportunity to count how many metric tons of force her body could produce.

"Soon, Mama," Dr. Sutherland said, pressing his hand on the glass to comfort her. "I promise I'm not stalling you. I can't take any risks of them coming in here and stopping us. Once they're all dead, we can leave."

Pain clenched his brains. The lampreys hiding in his gray matter dug their teeth in deeper. Mama doubted him and his ability to grant her safe passage off the installation.

"I swear to you I will keep you safe! I am your vessel! Let me serve you. I beg you!"

Dr. Sutherland could hear the wet squish of his brains. His limbs jerked in nervous responses. The lampreys under his flesh bit down, and Dr. Sutherland screeched, "*They won't come to stop us! By the time they show up, we'll be gone!*"

Biting down ever deeper into his brains, Dr. Sutherland was on hands and knees struggling to deal with the pain.

"You want out? Is that what you want? *I know, I know, I know, I know, I know*, you've waited so long. I haven't been stalling. I only want your safe passage to the United States. You're so very hungry. If you can't wait, then fine, but you must consume more meat first. You know what you need to do!"

Dr. Sutherland clutched his aching skull. "What now, Mama? What do you want from me? Make the pain stop!"

The doctor could sense what Mama was thinking. Images of his private lab flashed in his mind. He also saw Conrad wander into the secret lab.

"No! He must not disturb my work!"

Dr. Sutherland fled the room in pursuit of Conrad.

Chapter Thirty-Two

Henry moved swiftly and silently down each corridor. So far, he hadn't come upon a single lamprey. The blood drenching his body had long since gone cold. His adrenaline had spiked earlier, and now, it was declining. Exhaustion was setting in deep. There was no time to rest or replenish himself. Determination was hard to enforce in this situation, but that supply increased itself when he spotted a strange man lurking in the nearby corridor. He had exited a lab and was ambling towards a door. The man had lampreys sticking out of his exposed brains. He was chattering to himself things Henry couldn't understand.

He waited at the turn in the hallway. The doctor was inside the room for a while, and then he returned to the hallway. The door to the private room was slowly closing. Henry rushed it, slipped through the door, and entered. The doctor hadn't spotted him. He was too busy talking to himself to notice Henry.

Inside, Henry looked at every security monitor. The monitors showed every corridor. He saw Duke move in a strange laboratory full of broken glass displays. Scoop was moving in the shadows of a room he couldn't place. Dirty Poncho's badly mutilated body was dumping random appendages into a huge pile. Once the piles were tall enough, the lampreys from the ceiling stuck their sucker faces down to eat the human remains.

Henry knew little about the science behind the lampreys. One thing was obvious. A plan was being executed here. He could only guess they were scraping for food. And when that food ran out, what came next was escaping the installation in search of more sustenance. They would swim in the ocean and seek out more meat. Henry couldn't let that happen.

He searched for Conrad.

His son wasn't showing up in any of the feeds.

Conrad had to be dead.

Henry kept eyeballing the monitors. *Come on, son. Don't be dead. I couldn't live with myself if something happened to you.*

A multitude of things could've happened to his son. Conrad could be waiting outside the installation. Bavardi had forced him outside, so why not? There wasn't any camera feeds outside. That had to be it; Henry had to believe. He needed that spark of hope. Conrad could possibly be alive.

Henry found the naval radio. He could call for help. He decided to take a chance and call up ENTECH. Henry didn't have the full story yet on what was really going on. He had worked for ENTECH for nearly two decades, and they hadn't done him wrong before now. Henry understood things can change, but he still had to try. Anything was possible.

ENTECH replied immediately. Roger McCormick, a trusted contact at ENTECH, spoke to Henry.

"Forget the mission," Roger reported. "ENTECH has been bought out by TECHMODE. TECHMODE doesn't play by the rules of morality. Every project is being re-evaluated by TECHMODE. I'm hiding in the main office. Those TECHMODE deem unfit for duty are being executed. They'll find me soon, Henry. I'm so sorry I can't help you. Save yourself. Trust no one."

Henry begged Roger to explain the double cross, and the reason for this installation.

"All I know is PROJECT EV-180 PREY was originally started as an environmental cause. But the lampreys latched onto certain scientists, possessed them, and the lampreys took on a new life. Certain experiments took place because of this, and one of the lampreys has grown to enormous size. ENTECH wanted to pull the plug on the project to save lives, but when TECHMODE bought them out, they wanted to see what else the lampreys could accomplish on the installation. They're exploring other uses for PROJECT EV-180 PREY. They'll risk public contamination to make a profit.

"You can't let a single lamprey escape into the water. Oh no, I hear them coming. They've found me. I'm next to die. Save yourself. Kill every lamprey on that installation before it's too late. The fate of humanity is in your hands..."

Roger's response was cut off. He imagined what fate would befall his trusted contact at ENTECH.

Another voice picked up on the line.

"Your friend is dead, Henry Garfield. TECHMODE is your boss now. There is no more ENTECH. Keep those creatures busy. They need something to chew on until we figure out what the hell to do with them. We're still trying to figure out how to market them. You're putting on a good show. I've been watching the live feeds. The longer you survive, the longer the lampreys will stay on that installation. That's why we've been sending teams onto that rig. As long as they're fed, they have no reason to leave. So do as I say, and remember something. If the lampreys don't kill you, we will."

The line went dead.

Henry couldn't give up. He tried other channels. He reached out to anybody who would pick up.

There was only static.

Henry needed his team back together again, and fast.

The doctor was using this security room to speak to them via the intercom system. Henry decided to do the same. Henry heard his voice amplify throughout the vast corridors of the installation. He told whoever out there was still alive to meet him here in this wing.

Now Henry would sit tight, wait for his team, monitor the security feeds, and try to come up with a solid plan to kill every last lamprey on this rig.

Chapter Thirty-Three

I can't turn back now, Conrad kept telling himself. *There's no other way to go. I must search this room.* The room was horrible. He left the freezer only for something else to chill him. The lab was secreted from the rest of the installation. The walls were wood bared to the grain. Doorways were painted over and bolted with heavy duty locks. The smells in the room tested Conrad's gorge. Things lived and died in here. This was a testing room of some kind. Tables strewn with notebooks were covered in bloody fingerprints and laptop computers were grimy along the keyboards with blood and hunks of puckering flesh.

Conrad kept moving and searching for any other exit. He had no choice but to look at this chamber of horrors. A glass box contained a giant pink stomach. It was spliced in half so Conrad could see hundreds of teeth lining the inside of the stomach. Connected to the stomach was an elongated esophagus that led up several feet to a lamprey throat and sucker face.

Wooden pallets were stacked in a corner of the dank, disgusting room. Conrad read the label on one of the broken up crates that had been stacked on one of the pallets. The label was wet with humidity. The ink was smeared. He could only read a few of the words.

Live Cargo
Open Immediately

Broken crates were spread out on the floor. He read other partial labels. Many of them labeled variations of "Live Cargo" while others listed foreign countries. *China. Indonesia. Taiwan. Peru.*

There was one crate left on the pallet that was unopened. Conrad couldn't help but wonder what was inside of it. It was obvious once he grabbed a crowbar leaning up against the wall and smashed the damn thing open.

Within heavy plastic bags, he discovered torsos, appendages, and organs from human beings.

"*God-damn!*"

Conrad clutched the crowbar and retreated from the pallet and the body parts.

"Feed me," a voice said. "All you have to do is drop those body parts in my cage. It doesn't matter if they're rotting. My body can consume rancid meat. It won't hurt me. On the contrary, it'll be delicious. So just dump them in my cage. That's all I'm asking. I won't hurt you. I have no reason if I'm fed."

Conrad searched the room and couldn't pinpoint the voice. He weaved through steel gurneys with torsos of half bodies strapped down, the corpses gutted and limbless. Some dead bodies had lampreys trapped in their bodies, and those lampreys were rotting husks. They were failed experiments of some kind, Conrad imagined.

Black body bags were strewn on the floor. These were other human specimens. Corpses, Conrad thought. These scientists were trying to merge dead bodies with lampreys.

He imagined Bavardi up and walking, talking, and stalking him. Whoever made decisions here was one sick individual, he thought. Some advances in science came at too great a cost. The things in this room were truly sadistic.

That sadism didn't end with the bodies dead on stretchers, butchered, and surgically altered to allow lampreys too occupy their anatomies. There was a line of Plexiglas enclosures. Each was slathered in red, obscuring what was inside, except for one cage.

"Feed me," a woman said again. It was the same voice as earlier. Her body was covered in lampreys from top to bottom, their bodies crisscrossing each other. They looked like black amphibious rope, how the lampreys bodies hugged onto her body. "They're locked onto me like this for a reason. If I don't feed them soon, they'll feed on me. The scientists wanted to see how long the lampreys could survive without food, when they eat, how they choose to eat, and what parts of the body they prefer.

"Dr. Sutherland and his team turned on the interns. They used us for gruesome experiments. Dr. Sutherland replaced male and female reproductive organs with lamprey parts and forced them to have sex with each other. It was a bloodbath. They flew in dead human body parts to keep the lampreys fed. This project keeps costing more and more human life. I don't know what good can come of this—*ahhhhhgawwwd!*"

Lampreys bared down their sucker faces on her body. From head to toe, she was shredded, sucked, and devoured. Just like the rest of the Plexiglas fronts, hers was also slathered in blood.

Conrad bumped into a wire cage with a man hunkered down chewing on dead lamprey bodies. His face was covered in the putrid black jellies of lamprey innards. The human-turned- savage hissed at Conrad, and then went back to devouring the lamprey bodies. The man was digging into a deep trough of dead lamprey bodies and feasting.

He couldn't take anymore. Conrad did his best to avoid details of the room. He only focused on finding another doorway. Conrad located one, opened it, and wandered down a hallway, made two right turns, and he opened the next door he located. It turned out to be a conference room. And a familiar person was waiting inside.

Scoop.

Chapter Thirty-Four

Duke couldn't believe he was following after Bavardi. Bavardi had cleared the way of the dead scientists just moments ago. Even in death, Bavardi could kick some ass. Duke was still reeling at the sight of Bavardi. The man's body was infested with lampreys. The sound of the wet bodies occupying tissue and bone was sickening enough. On top of that, Bavardi was fighting a battle in his mind. He kept growling, cursing, and clenching his face and arms in nervous spasms.

"They're trying to control me," Bavardi said through clenched teeth. They turned down another hallway. "I will beat them. They don't realize what I've been through. They don't know the power of my mind."

Before Duke could say anything to Bavardi, the man pointed at a steel door. "Your father is in there. That's where he made the report over the intercom. The lampreys know all. They look into me, and I see into them. I have things to do if I'm going to save your lives."

Bavardi turned in the opposite direction.

"Wait, where are you going? You don't have to fight this alone. Something can be done to help you."

When he said that, Duke knew it was a lie. The man was badly mutilated. It was a miracle, or an abomination, of science, that Bavardi still existed.

"I'm going to stop Mama."

Duke didn't know what to say to Bavardi's comment. He didn't have time to ask him who "Mama" was. He let Bavardi go his way. Duke approached the door and knocked. When the door opened, his father greeted him with open arms.

I am not your vessel.

I am a lamprey killing machine.

Bavardi snuck into the lab where Mama stirred in her tank. She knew he was in the room, and there was nothing Mama could do.

My mind is stronger than you.
I am going to kill you right here.
Go suck yourself in hell.

Dr. Sutherland wasn't in the lab. Bavardi wasn't sure where the man had disappeared to, but this was his chance to end the situation. He knew if Mama was stopped, the rest of the lampreys wouldn't know what to do. Mama was their queen. Kill the queen, the servants die with her. The lampreys were no different from ants.

Bavardi could climb to the top of the stairway into Mama's enclosure, but he couldn't reach the ceiling. He would have to do something insane to kill Mama.

He imagined it, and his body followed the commands. Both of his arms unlocked from his body, propelled by the lampreys under his command. Those arms slithered across the floor, up the wall, and climbed to the ceiling. The arms tore through the paneling walls and exposed thick black rubber electrical wires. The arms and lamprey suckers worked in tandem to rip those cables from the ceiling. The frayed ends of the cables were shedding blue sparks. Those cables dropped into Mama's tank.

Mama sensed trouble. She thrashed unseen in the dark waters. Waves crashed, spilling water over the top. The second the wires touched down, the water boiled, jolted with staggering amounts of electricity.

Fry Mama, you bitch!

Chapter Thirty-Five

Conrad shut the door behind him, blocked it with a long conference table, and hurried over to Scoop. She lay on the ground. Her uniform was covered in blood and she smelled of heavy smoke. She was happy to see him. He offered to help her up, but she wanted him to sit down next to her.

"Are you hurt?"

Scoop nodded. "I've been running from room to room avoiding those things. I used the duct systems when I dropped down into this room, and my ankle gave out on me. I can't run. If I can't run, I might as well be dead."

"No, don't talk like that. If I've made it this long, you can survive easy, bad ankle or not."

Scoop seemed loopy. She noticed Conrad look at her funny. "Yeah, I took a pain pill. I'm a little funny in the head, but I can still focus. The pill loosens me up, that's all."

"I could use a pill or two," Conrad said. "Don't go out there, by the way. There's some sick shit going on. Whoever is running this place, they've done some experiments that go far beyond wrong. Insanity's a good word."

Scoop put her hand on the back of Conrad's head. "Your brother talked about you a lot. He said you were a pansy and you weren't cut out for the military. I say who cares. I don't like that machismo bullshit. Life shouldn't be a pissing contest. Every guy I've met in the service wants to talk about how big their dick is and how far it can piss. You seem modest to me. I like a man with a brain. He can teach me things, and I can teach him things."

Conrad hadn't been touched by a woman since before his wedding disaster with Arielle. And Arielle never looked at Conrad like Scoop was eyeballing him. Those eyes were enticing, and Scoop's voice was silken lust.

He knew it was the pain pill she'd taken and the situation. When faced with death, social filters were removed. Any guy looked enticing. And Conrad was that guy.

"I heard about your ex," Scoop said. "She sounds like a real bitch. You're handsome, and you seem like a nice kind of guy. You're trusting. Anybody who's been cheated on like that is trusting. It means you're not afraid to open up your heart to someone. Machismo guys don't know how to do that, but you, Conrad, I bet you'd make a great lover.

"Fuck it, Conrad. There's a good chance we're going to die here. I haven't been laid by a good man in a long time. A *l-ooong* time. I can do things to your dick you wouldn't believe. I can hold my breath for a very long time."

"Huh? Why would you need to hold your breath? What kind of a pill did you take exactly?"

Scoop wasn't hearing him. She was stroking the back of his head and purring under her breath. "I'll tell you about things you never thought about trying. You ever stick your balls in a woman's pussy? You can stick them in mine. It'll make us both feel so good."

"But wouldn't that hurt? I mean, wouldn't it hurt my nuts? Why would I do that? I'm so confused."

From behind the door, Conrad heard a madman rage. Conrad was sent from one extreme moment to the next without time to process anything.

"*So you found my private laboratory? I had to come here and make sure you didn't ruin any of my research. I don't have cameras in this wing, but I know you're in there. I can smell your flesh.* ATTACK! KILL THEM ALL!"

The door was kicked, shredded, and decimated by lampreys of every size. The walls, up from the floor, the ceiling, everywhere was bursting into pieces. Hundreds of sucker maws were preparing to suck them into their hungry mouths. Suctions of air batted at them from all directions. The air streams threw Conrad and Scoop about the room, tossing them like street litter. Conrad clutched onto Scoop, fearing her drugged state would allow her to fly right into one of their deadly mouths. The wild suctions of air caused the ground to come undone beneath them. Conrad and Scoop plummeted down.

The drop wasn't far.

They hit a series of emergency stairs.

Conrad helped Scoop to her feet. She couldn't balance on one foot due to her ankle, so Conrad picked her up in his arms. He unleashed a battle cry. He read somewhere in a health magazine that if you yelled, your body sent energy to your muscles. Conrad kept releasing yawps and growls as he carried Scoop to somewhere else.

The lampreys were slithering down from the holes in the ceiling. The deadly lamprey rain kept Conrad moving. He had little time to think when a new hole formed in the ceiling. Steel was peeled back, and a giant lamprey mouth hissed and drooled pelting sheets of rubber glue saliva down onto them. Scoop was terrified. Conrad didn't waste a minute to defend themselves.

Conrad spotted the axe in the emergency case. He smashed it open with his elbow. He clutched the axe, reached down to help up Scoop to her feet, when the beast in the ceiling sucked them up into its maw. They were drawn through the ceiling to the roof of the building. Scoop landed on the roof, falling from the mouth. Conrad remained in the beast's mouth. He had his legs braced so the beast couldn't swallow him down. The mouth was contracting and trying to suck him down. Conrad's feet were slipping. He wouldn't be able to hold on much longer before the monster swallowed him.

Conrad used the axe to hack into the soft fleshy material that covered the roof of its mouth. After hacking for minutes and holding on for his life, he threw the axe down the lamprey's throat and crawled up through the slit he created and slipped down its slimy body and onto the roof. Scoop gawked at him in amazement. She couldn't believe he'd survived.

"Come on, we've got to move! No time to sit and stare!"

Conrad picked her up in his arms again. They were on the move. It was still dark outside. The ocean was vast. Nobody knew what was happening here. They were on their own.

The giant lamprey was after them, snaking across the roof. He could hear the *crick-crack-crick-crack-crick-crack-crick-crack* of spinning teeth. Large tracks of the roof were peeled and ripped. Their roof was coming undone. Conrad had to watch his steps as flying debris sailed past them. He imagined a tornado staying low to the ground.

Scoop was getting heavy in his arms. Every step he took threatened to drop him to the ground. If he stopped weaving and dodging the suction force of the lamprey charging behind him for one second, it'd be guaranteed death.

He got lucky earlier with that axe trick.

That luck wouldn't happen again.

Thinking about his luck, it suddenly ran out. Before he could stop, there was nowhere else to escape. The roof was in shreds, and he couldn't stop himself before they dropped down into the gaping wide hole ahead of them. They fell back into the installation. They landed hard shortly after the fall. Conrad knew where they'd fallen immediately.

He'd been here before.

The huge aquarium.

The steel platform.

Conrad knew they had to get moving, and fast. Lampreys were slithering down from the hole they'd created. He helped Scoop up. She was dazed and slow. Conrad kept encouraging her to get up and fight. Conrad used himself as her crutch again, and they hurried down the stairs together.

"Son! You're alive!"

Henry was below with Duke. Conrad hurried towards them. When they met up, Bavardi was standing near them. He was strange looking to begin with, but now he had no arms. From the ceiling, the two arms crawled back down and re-connected themselves to Bavardi's shoulder sockets with the help of working lampreys.

"That's insane," was all Conrad could say.

"He won't hurt you," Henry said. "Bavardi's on our side. Without him, we'd all be dead. He fried that monster in the cage. She turned into one crispy bitch. They won't hurt us now. Without their leader, they're nothing."

"You don't understand," Conrad argued. "They're coming down after us. Hordes of them. Look!"

"But I killed Mama," Bavardi insisted. "Without her, they're useless."

Dr. Sutherland stormed into the room. He threw his head back and cackled. "You didn't kill Mama. She's very much alive! She's going to bloom. Nobody can stop her! NOW YOU SHALL BE DEVOURED!"

Chapter Thirty-Six

Suction force threw Conrad and the rest of them off of their feet and to the other side of the room. Conrad held onto Scoop. They had no chance of fighting what arrived. Hundreds of lampreys poured from the ceiling, escaped from the grates in the wall, and slithered in long lines through the double doors of the laboratory. The lampreys would team up and feast upon them.

Dr. Sutherland was standing across from them witnessing the mass entry of eel-bodied, sucker-faced monsters. He was cheering. "*Feed her. She needs her strength. Our souls will live on. Your flesh and blood will be one. Through her, you will be consumed and then reborn. Forever, you shall feast on flesh and consume to your infernal insatiable desires!*"

Conrad heard the water sloshing in the giant water tank. A body pressed against the glass, bashing itself until long spider-web cracks formed. Then all at once, the glass tank shattered. Water spilled forth, spewing out a tidal wave. Dr. Sutherland was swept off of his feet and submerged in the water.

Henry shouted, "Grab hold of something before the water sucks you in!"

Conrad had hold of Scoop with one arm and the other clutched onto a steel table leg nailed into the floor. When the great wave of water hit him, the force made him release Scoop.

"No! Scoop!"

The water swallowed her up out of sight. Henry, Duke, and Bavardi were also gone. No time to think. Conrad clutched onto the steel table leg and tried to keep his head above water. As fast as the wave swept everybody away, the waters thinned out.

Conrad stayed where he was when he saw the beast rise from the broken aquarium.

Mama had to weigh many tons. Her gaping sucker face was three stories high. He imagined a fat caterpillar spray-painted black. Each individual tooth could impale three people. When the teeth spun, the collective suction force drew in every lamprey beast into her sucker face. The spinning of blades sounded like a mega helicopter about to take flight. When the bodies hit her teeth, it was a booming garbage disposal of clicks, snaps, breaking, and liquefaction.

The zombie-fied scientists were sucked up into the mouth along with the subjects for the experiments gone wrong. The leftover piles of body parts the undead drones hadn't collected flew into the room. Conrad's eyes widened as he watched flying arms, hands, and gusts spinning and colliding into Mama's teeth. He understood why the lamprey would eat the humans, but why her own kind?

The smaller lampreys were like bicycle streamers catching air as they were drawn into Mama's hideous maw. The larger lampreys took longer to be driven through her teeth; seconds instead of instantly. Mama's sucker face was a flood of dribbling blood. Out her back side, broken bones was shit out as such speeds and force they tore through steel and ended up in another room or landed in the ocean.

The roar of spinning teeth ended. Mama slumped down into herself and breathed hard. Every intake was a rumble and quake.

Conrad couldn't understand what she was doing. Why did she stop eating? Was she sleeping? Henry, Duke, and Scoop were spread out on the floor unconscious. Conrad made sure they were still breathing. They were breathing and very much alive.

He wasn't sure what happened to Bavardi. Conrad imaged the poor son-of-a-bitch was sucked into that maw and eaten like the rest of the human experiments gone wrong.

"Wake up," Conrad said, shaking his father. "I need you. Please. I can't do this alone."

Conrad tried to rouse everyone, and nobody woke.

He remembered back at his apartment when his father and brother asked him to take a volunteer trip to Africa. When Conrad asked them why they kept the secret from him, Duke said, *"Because, brother, you're kind of a wimp."*

Conrad had survived this long. Why couldn't he survive the situation altogether? He would save them from death, and from now on, nobody could say shit about Conrad and his love of books and the English language, because at one point in time, he had saved them from being eaten by one huge ugly lamprey bitch.

Conrad couldn't wait to tell his mom the story.

She would be so proud of him.

Think. How do I get them out of this room? If they stay in here, that thing will wake up and start eating again.

The giant monster was breathing hard.

Mama wasn't moving.

It appeared she was in fact sleeping.

Conrad searched the room. He didn't have a plan to save anybody until his eyes found the pushcart nearby. The aquarium's water must've washed it up from its hiding place. Conrad imagined Dr. Sutherland using the cart to wheel in heaps of body parts and gore to feed that ugly thing.

Get moving.

You can't stay in this room another minute.

Conrad rushed to the task. He hefted Scoop across the room and placed her on the cart. Duke was heavier. He had to drag his brother by the legs and lift him up onto the cart top half first, bottom half last. Conrad lifted up his father, kicking out one great burst of energy to move him quickly.

Before he could push the cart out of the room, Dr. Sutherland stood in the way of the door.

Chapter Thirty-Seven

Dr. Sutherland beheld Mama from a distance.

"She's metabolizing what she's consumed. Give her a few more minutes, and she'll wake. I can hear her organs churning the meat and turning it into fuel.

"My colleagues thought I was crazy when the lampreys entered my body. They tried to put me in a cage and lock me up. They couldn't contain me, just like they couldn't contain the others. I don't understand why they thought I was crazy, or that I wouldn't be rewarded for my service. They were so wrong. Everything is paying off."

Dr. Sutherland's eyes rolled into his skull. Teeth sprouted around the gummy tissue of his sockets. "I stand tall among the lampreys! I will see the end of the human race. I will be a king."

Conrad was terrified of the doctor. "What happens when they eat everything? When you've wiped out the human race, what will be left to consume? You ever think about that?"

Dr. Sutherland didn't like the question. The lampreys buried in his brains surfaced, rising up like spitting vipers. He lifted up his midsection, displaying that grotesque mouth. Teeth spun in the man's midsection.

"I'm going to eat you for speaking such insolence!"

Dr. Sutherland charged after him. Conrad thought about turning the other way and running, but he couldn't leave his fallen comrades behind.

Then he remembered something.

His vest!

He forgot he'd been wearing the damn thing this whole time. Amati had given it to him back at Conrad's apartment.

Dr. Sutherland was almost on him. Conrad unbuttoned the first pocket, dug his fingers in, and grabbed the first thing he could retrieve. He held it up to Dr. Sutherland's hideous mouth-eyes and dosed the lunatic with a jet of pepper spray.

Foam sizzled and dribbled down the wailing doctor's face. It slowed him down, but it didn't stop him. He had to do something else.

"I'm going to eat you! The pain in my eyes, you will feel thirty fold in your entire body. I will devour you slowly, piece by piece, ounce by ounce, I will—"

Conrad maced the doctor's exposed brain and watched the surface fizz with red foamy blood. The individual lampreys on the doctor's head hid back into Dr. Sutherland's brain in retreat. The doctor stumbled to the ground wailing in agony.

He didn't know how long Dr. Sutherland would be incapacitated, so now was the time to act. Conrad raced back to the pushcart. Now was his chance to escape the room with his life and his friends. Using every ounce of strength left in his body, Conrad shoved the cart forward. When he crossed the threshold, Mama was finished metabolizing the mass of meat she'd consumed.

Chapter Thirty-Eight

Conrad saw Mama wake. She opened that enormous maw and unleashed a thunderous growl of hunger. "She rises!" Dr. Sutherland declared as bloody tears trailed from his eyes and thick syrupy blood oozed from his brains. "Long live Mama—!"

Dr. Sutherland's body blew up from the powerful suction force of Mama's mouth. He was liquid before he touched those razor teeth. The sight of his air mutilation sent Conrad pushing the cart out of the room with renewed energy.

Mama erupted at his escape. He imagined a motorized fan the size of a city kicking up insane wind speeds. Those speeds seemed to chew up the walls of an entire section of the building. Roaring harder, the suction power peeled back the roof. He imagined the top of a sardine can being pulled back by a giant. A long sliver of dawn's light poured into the building.

Move faster. She's going to tear you a new one. She's going to tear everybody a fucking new one!

Up ahead, an access door opened by itself.

What the hell?

Bavardi's voice spoke into the intercom. "Move your ass, soldier. This mission isn't completed yet. The bitch stills breathes!"

Conrad couldn't believe the man who almost beat him to death back at that seedy hotel room would be his savior.

He pushed the cart through the open steel door. When he crossed the access, the steel door closed.

Conrad was pushing the cart across a narrow hallway. Glass formed a half dome shape overhead. Another steel door opened up ahead of him. Bavardi had snuck off to one of the security rooms. The guy was quick thinking and resourceful, even when he was infested by lampreys. Conrad could only imagine what the guy had accomplished in the field of combat. No wonder his father wanted him as a Post-Service Operative.

Once he crossed the door, and he'd pushed the cart through, the door wanted to close, but the mechanism was stuck.

"Sorry, Conrad," Bavardi said over the intercom. "It still buys you time. The outside door is open. You can reach the outside landing. I don't know what you can do from there. I'll try to help you. But you're on your own until I can reach you."

Conrad stood there watching Henry, Duke, and Scoop lay there unconscious on the cart. He was in a room without much of anything inside of it. He noticed the two large steel boxes. One was empty, while the other one had—

The door across the long hallway was wrenched off the hinges and sucked back into the building. Conrad gasped seeing the giant mouth stick through the door and beginning to suction air. Conrad felt the tug on his skin. It could rip his flesh and dismantle him in moments.

He had to do something.

Conrad had one last idea to save his ass.

Chapter Thirty-Nine

Mama's mouth was all that could be seen through the access door. Saliva flooded forth in rubber glue torrents towards Conrad's feet. Mama was ready to feed. Conrad stood across the hallway facing the beast. He clutched the only remaining Gatling gun in the steel box with both hands. The weapon was heavy, and he wasn't sure if he was using it right, but what did he have to lose?

Conrad aimed the Gatling gun so he could send a torrent of bullets at the mouth. He imagined Mama to be the cat looking in at the mouse. When Conrad pulled back the trigger, he slipped in the goopy saliva covering the floor. He slammed into the ground with bullets spattering the ceiling. Broken glass windows shattered in every direction. Those reflective daggers were drawn into Mama's mouth. Once those shards hit home, blood spewed from Mama's sucker face.

"Yeah, suck on that shit! That make you bleed? *Then let's make you bleed.*"

Conrad blasted every glass pane. Glass was sucked up into the maw at vortex speeds. The effort was rewarded by more blasts and spraying geysers of blood.

"*Fuck you! Eat glass, lamprey whore!*"

Mama's cries sounded like a pontoon boat motor being sent through a meat grinder. Piercing and shrill screams hit Conrad so hard, he dropped the gun and cupped his ears. By then it was too late to brace for what was coming.

A red torrent of blood was coming right his way. A literal flood of blood, the crimson tidal wave was fast approaching.

Conrad was lapped up, lifted up off of his feet, and spun upside down and right side up until he was too disoriented to compute what was occurring. Red became everything. He couldn't breathe. He was forced under the insane red tide.

Conrad reached out for purchase. Somehow, he'd been delivered straight out of the installation, across the helipad, and onto the edge of the rig. He was clutching onto the very edge of the platform to save his life. Conrad was weak, dizzy, and still processing the moment.

His hold was slipping.

He was seconds from falling into the ocean.

Chapter Forty

Conrad couldn't hold on anymore. Blood was pouring over the edge of the platform and pelting him in the face. His eyes were stinging. The grip on the steel was too slick to stay strong. Conrad fought on for as long as he could when his fingers made the decision for him.

He let go.

Conrad closed his eyes. He wondered how long the fall would take. Would he drop straight down, or would he bob on the surface of the ocean and struggle for air until his body was so weak, he let himself go under and die?

"I got you!"

Duke had him by the arm.

His brother lifted him back up to the platform.

"Close call, bro," Duke said, patting him on the back hard. "You're not half the pussy I thought you to be. I don't know what you did to that beast to make it bleed like that. That's amazing. Now all we have to do is figure out a way off of this rig."

Conrad joined Duke in walking across the platform and helping Henry and Scoop up to their feet. They were disoriented and confused, but also conscious. Henry kept clutching his head, as did Scoop. She still couldn't stand without help.

"The naval radio should still work," Henry said. "We'll see if we can reach out to anybody who can pick us up. If not, we've got two helicopters right here. We can fly one of them back to land. I prefer to take the one without two festering corpses in the front seat."

"What about ENTECH?" Duke asked.

"They can't be trusted anymore," Henry said. "I got hold of ENTECH over the radio earlier. They've been bought out by somebody else. We might have to turn to the United States government. If that doesn't work, maybe we can be granted asylum in another country until this blows over."

Conrad couldn't believe what he was hearing. He imagined hiding in a foreign country, or having to always be on the run from some evil empire who didn't want them to leak the secrets of lamprey research.

"Whatever happens, all I want is a hot shower," Scoop said. "And some chili fries."

The group laughed.

Then they cried out in horror.

The roof over the installation nearest them was ripped off. Mama's body surged from the opening. She was gigantic and standing tall like a cobra snake. Her sucker face and body was covered in dangling ribbons of broken flesh. Her motor teeth still functioned, spinning and creating suction force. Conrad had only slowed the monster; he hadn't destroyed it.

"Hold on," Henry said. "The bitch ain't dead yet."

"We can't let her escape," Duke said. "If she drops into the water, she'll head straight for land."

Conrad felt his feet leave the ground. Scoop collapsed and was about to be dragged in the hideous bleeding lamprey beast's mouth.

Henry and Duke were struggling to keep their feet planted on the ground. Mama battered her bulky body into the sides of the building until the structure was gone. Her black eel body gleamed in the sun. Beneath the serrated and torn flaps of skin, Conrad could see clear gelatinous eggs. There were thousands and thousands of eggs.

Conrad couldn't let Mama take the plunge off the platform and into the ocean.

He crawled, spun, and shot up to his feet. He ran right for the helicopter with the machine gun turrets. Conrad shoved aside one of the corpses in the seat. He searched the panel for an on switch. He couldn't decide what would turn the engine on. It didn't take long to realize he didn't know a goddamn thing about helicopters.

"Fuck! How do I start this thing?"

One of the corpses shifted in the passenger seat. Conrad gasped, wondering if another corpse had been inhabited by lampreys. It turned out to be Bavardi. He stepped into the helicopter.

"Time for me to take over," Bavardi said, edging Conrad out of the driver's seat. "I'm as good as dead. You save your friends over there. This is one-way death ride. Now move out!"

Conrad jumped from the chopper right when it started up. Bavardi released a wall of gunfire from the turrets. Mama stopped suctioning once those bullets hit home.

Bavardi spoke from the helicopter's bullhorn. "Forgive me, Henry, for betraying you. Let me make it up to you. I'm sending this bitch packing to hell!"

Conrad hit the deck.

Bavardi crashed the helicopter right into Mama's mouth. A great incendiary explosion rocked the platform. A mean ball of flames ate at Mama's face. Melting flesh, broken up spinning teeth, chunks of meat flying, and lamprey guts rained down in hundred pound heaps. After the debris settled, a line of helicopters was fast approaching the installation. Conrad stood next to his father, brother, and Scoop, and waited to find out who was coming.

Chapter Forty-One

Five helicopters touched down. Men in white hazmat suits armed with flamethrowers torched the remains of Mama's body. The rest of the crew stormed into the facility, blanketing everything from top to bottom in fire. Henry, Duke, and Scoop were taken into custody and forced into a helicopter. Conrad was handcuffed from behind and forced into a different helicopter.

"Stay calm, son," Henry shouted at Conrad. "You let me figure this out. You sit tight. We survived this bullshit; we'll survive a little bit more."

Conrad waited in the chopper while the unknown team secured the installation. After an hour, the helicopter took flight. He was being taken to a place yet to be determined. Hours later, the helicopter dropped them off on a landing pad in front of a military building. Conrad was delivered to a holding cell and stayed there alone.

He was allowed a shower, given a change of clothes, and a meal that tasted like a frozen dinner zapped in a microwave. Conrad waited for hours, and when the cell's door opened, he was surprised. Henry and Duke greeted him. They too had had a change of clothing, some food, and a new disposition.

"Everything's going to okay," Henry reassured his son. "The team that picked us up isn't from ENTECH, and they're not TECHMODE either. Both of them are bad guys now. I guess creating terrorist weapons is far more lucrative than saving the environment. Things change and they sure change fast."

Conrad was confused. "Then who picked us up? How do we know they're good?"

Duke smiled. "We know they're good because they torched a multi-million dollar project without batting an eye."

Henry agreed. "This new group is called AGRO-CORE. They're a very different kind of fighting force. They deal in situations involving...how shall I put it? Monsters. AGRO-CORE has hired us to lead a new team into various foreign countries to clean up or prevent research of this kind from spiraling out of control. We can't talk much about it to you, son, I'm afraid. They're letting you go. You have to sign a few waivers, saying you want say a word of this to anybody."

"Like anyone would believe me if I did," Conrad said. "So just like that, you're playing on a new team."

"Other Post-Service Operatives have done the same," Henry explained. "Like I said, things change. That's life. How you deal with the changes makes you who you are."

Duke hugged Conrad. "I'm sorry I gave you such a hard time all of these years. You saved our lives. You were very brave under harsh circumstances. Are you sure you don't want to join in the effort?"

Conrad didn't have to think about it. "I don't think so. While I was running from sucker-faced monsters, I realized I made a mistake. I mean about quitting my job. I love being an English professor. I might have to wait until next semester, but I'm getting that job back. Arielle can go to hell. I'm over the tramp. She can have her cake and fuck it too."

"That's my boy," Henry said. "Wait until your mom hears about this. She'll be so proud."

They talked a little more about the future, and the plans for their next family get-together.

Before they said their goodbyes and Conrad would be shipped back home, Duke smiled at his brother.

"You have a special visitor. We'll leave you two alone."

Scoop entered the room on crutches. She put the crutches up against the wall and sat next to Conrad on the cot. Scoop put her arm around Conrad and kissed his neck. "We don't have much time before I have to get moving. Take off your pants, handsome. You remember what I promised to do to your balls back when we were alone together?"

Conrad forgot about everything that had happened to him in the last forty-eight hours in the span of ten minutes.

Epilogue

Conrad faced a new semester of students at Texas University. He was surprised how his old colleagues vouched for him and helped him get his job back. Arielle was fired for having an inappropriate relationship with a student during the semester Conrad was unemployed. That didn't surprise Conrad. Everything had fallen back into place ever since the horrors he faced defeating the lampreys. His family was fighting God knew what, God knew where, and Conrad was here on campus conducting a literature class.

The book the class was to discuss today was *Moby Dick*.

It was the early morning class, and most of his students had either dragged themselves out of bed, were hung over, or waiting for their coffee fix to kick in. Conrad was doing most of the talking, when one student let out a comment.

"How could you capture and kill a whale back in the day? Seriously? It would be impossible. It's hard enough now with the current technology. One man can't beat a whale. It's impossible. It's the strongest sea creature of them all."

Conrad couldn't help but correct the lame-brain student. "A whale's not the strongest sea creature of them all."

"Then what's stronger than a whale, Professor?"

Conrad woke up the whole class with his booming voice.

"Try going up against some motherfucking lampreys!"

The End